THE
RETURN

THE
RETURN

by SONIA LEVITIN

Atheneum   1987   New York

Atheneum
Macmillan Publishing Company
866 Third Avenue, New York, NY 10022

Type set by Arcata Graphics/Kingsport, Kingsport Tennessee
Printed and bound by Fairfield Graphics, Fairfield, Pennsylvania
Designed by Marjorie Zaum
Map by Felicia Bond
First Edition

10   9   8   7   6   5   4   3   2   1

Library of Congress Cataloging-in-Publication Data

Levitin, Sonia
The return.

Bibliography: p.
SUMMARY: Desta and the other members of her Falasha family, Jews suffering
from discrimination in Ethiopia, finally flee the country and attempt
the dangerous journey to Israel.
[1. Falashas—Fiction.   2. Jews—Ethiopia—Fiction.
3. Antisemitism—Fiction.   4. Prejudices—Fiction.
5. Ethiopia—Fiction]   I. Title.
PZ7.L58Re   1987   [Fic]   86-25891
ISBN 0-689-31309-8

To Barbara Ribakove
"A woman of valour . . .
And let her works praise her."

A glossary of
italicized Amharic words
appears at the end
of the book.

ACKNOWLEDGMENTS

My heartfelt thanks to the following persons, who helped me immeasurably in the preparation for this book, giving their time and talents, knowledge and encouragement:

Chaim Aron, Jewish Agency, Israel, Head of Absorption Department
Lynne and Uri Bar-Ner of Jerusalem, for their hospitality and insights
Soshana Ben-Dor of the Ben Zvi Institute for ethnological material and
    information on religious practices
Louis Boorstin, former relief worker in Sudan
Friedl Cohen of Hofim Youth Village, Israel
Schmuel Danino, Director of Talpiot Youth Village, Israel
Yitzhak Eldan, Deputy Consul General of Israel, Los Angeles
Jane Fellman, American Association for Ethiopian Jews, Los Angeles
Avraham Freiman, Jewish Agency, Israel
Middie and Richard Giesberg, Los Angeles
Ted Kanner, Executive Director, Jewish Federation Council, Los Angeles
Marty Karp, Jewish Federation Council, Jerusalem
Ray Levine, Jewish Agency, Jerusalem
Clifford May, foreign correspondent, the *New York Times*
Marilyn and Robert McIntyre, Los Angeles
Rabbi Yosef Miller, Netanya, Israel
Dr. Chaim Peri, director of Yemin Orde, Israel
Louis Rapoport, Senior Editor, the *Jerusalem Post*
Barbara Ribakove, Founder and Director of NACOEJ, North American
    Conference on Ethiopian Jewry, New York
Marriam Cramer Ring, photographer, San Francisco
Allen Schwartz, NACOEJ, Jerusalem
Zweig Stanislovski, Director of Neve Armiel Youth Village, Israel
Barry Weise, former Director of ORT schools in Ethiopia
And an Ethiopian gentleman who wishes to be known only by his Hebrew
    name, Nataniel, as he fears reprisals against his kin remaining in exile.

Lastly, my thanks and deepest love to my husband, Lloyd, for encouraging me in this venture, and to my children, Dan and Shari, who accompanied me to see the Beta Yisrael.

S.L.

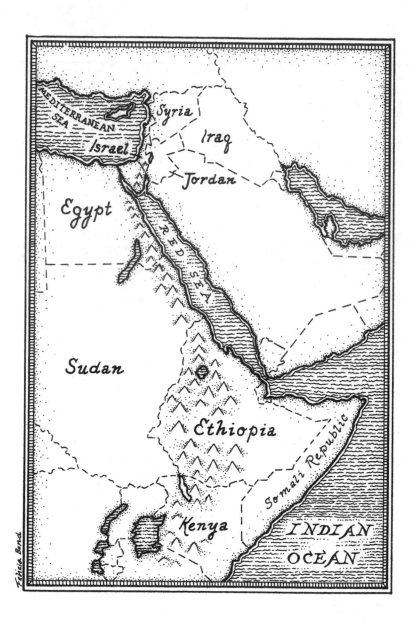

THE
RETURN

1

THERE IS A SMALL VILLAGE HIGH IN THE MOUNTAINS OF ETHIO-
pia. I can't tell you its name. But often I dream of my village
high in the Simien mountains, and when I wake up my face
is wet with tears.

In the dream I stand with my *shamma* wrapped tightly
around me, for the wind is chill. I wait for someone—perhaps
for the spirits of my mother and father, both dead, to lead
me away. I hear the sudden loud call of an eagle, and I
cannot decide: Shall I follow? Or shall I stay? How can I
leave my home and those I love?

In the dream I see everything clearly. The mountains
are blue-green in the distance. White mist clings to them in
early morning. A dirt road leads to our synagogue, a fine
building with a real tin roof and a star on top, made by our
own blacksmiths. Now the government has locked up our
synagogues and schools. They have taken away the keys.
They oppress us—you will see. Why else would we have
left our homes that were so beautiful?

Plain they were, but ours, built with our own hands. In my dreams I see the cluster of *tukels*, the round thatched huts where we lived. Beyond are fields for our crops and some pasture for the goats and sheep and a horse or two.

There is the hut of Gola, the weaver. Dug into the ground is a deep hole where Gola sits, his feet in the hole and threads attached to his great toes, the loom all around him, and the shuttle flying so!

I wonder if Gola is still there. By now many Jews have left their villages hoping to get to Israel. Not all of us got out. Some are still prisoners in Ethiopia.

Some people think we left Ethiopia because of the famine. No. Famine and drought oppress Africa, for sure, but in the mountains where we lived there was still some rain, and a few crops growing. It was not hunger that sent us away. We left for freedom, and because we were Jews, *Beta Yisrael*. The other tribes hated us, called us Falasha, stranger.

Why? I asked my Uncle Tekle. He shook his head, pausing in the hammer blows for he is a blacksmith, you see, with powerful arms, though his legs are knobby and weak from what those devils did to him.

"Desta, Desta," he murmured, gazing at me. "For a girl, you ask many questions; Auntie gets annoyed. Well, you should know it. There was a revolution here, when you were small. Our emperor—you know his name, eh? Haile Selassie? Well, he was never a real friend to Jews, so not much was lost for us. But the new *Dergue* is even worse. Communists." Uncle Tekle spat. He hates the communists as much as he hates the devils who beat him. "They said they would bring order. Reform." Again, he spat. "So they

4

came in with their tanks and guns," Uncle Tekle continued. He gazed at the metal plow point he was mending. He also knows how to make parts for rifles. "They mowed down everybody in their way. Thank God we did not see it! They called it the Red Terror. The streets of Addis Ababa ran red with blood."

"Tekle!" my aunt came scolding, hands on hips. "What things are you drumming into the head of this child? Desta, come to the fields, away from this man and his thundering. Come, we'll gather the *gesho* leaves for our brew. Tekle! Leave the child her innocence, at least for now."

My auntie stroked my head, kissed my cheek. "You need know nothing of these horrors, my lovely one," she said.

"Uncle told me they murdered teachers. Students. Even children."

"Well, well, but that is over now, and we have work to do." My pretty aunt frowned, then puffed out her long skirt of white homespun. "It is not good to think too much of the past, or of sorrow. Every day brings its work and its blessings."

"It was no blessing," I muttered, "the day the Dergue came in and murdered children."

"Enough!" my aunt said sharply, her lips pursed tight.

Well, you may ask, up high in the mountains, what had all this talk of revolution and killing to do with me? I was content, felt nothing strange; I remember how I used to love running in the fields. I remember how the ground looked after the long rains. Tall green grass covered the hillsides; our huts were nearly hidden by the high growth of maize all around, and small yellow daisies bloomed everywhere. After the rains the countryside was bright with acacia, berry bushes, laurel and mimosa. Women walked proud, arms swinging and with bundles on their heads, calling out, "Hello! What news?" and stopping to talk.

Now and then you could see a bushy-haired baboon playing between the trees, upright like a man. Donkeys roamed free, and cattle, too. That is strange, isn't it? In Ethiopia the animals go free, but some people are fettered, as we were in our own mountain homes.

It was against the law for us to leave Ethiopia. They hated us, but would not let us go.

Sometimes missionaries came to our villages, and later, even the *shum*, from the Peasants' Association, shouting, "Jews! You make yourselves ridiculous, with your prayer shawls and your yammering chants. Look about you! You are alone and destitute, a dying race. Why not join the rest of humanity? Accept the cross! You will be treated like men, then, instead of like vermin. Accept the cross!"

Many did. Others refused, and were killed. So we were indeed a dying race, only a few thousand where once we had been a million and strong.

Of course, it took a sign. That is always the way. Things can worsen for years, each little trouble seeming small and bearable. Then comes a sign, maybe in the form of a dream. Or a visit from a stranger. We had both.

It began one morning in early spring, with men in the fields, Aunt Kibret outside kneading clay for pots, everybody busy. The smell of coffee beans was in the air, for someone was grinding them fine. You could hear the wheeze of the bellows and hear the clink of my uncle's hammer. Joas worked with him, counting the strokes loudly. I was in the lean-to, grinding *teff* into the soft flour needed for our bread.

"*Sille!* Hurrah! *Sille!*" My little sister Almaz came running, shouting over the sound of our work. "Desta, it is Dan," Almaz cried. "Hurry! Go and wash your hands and face. Hurry!"

I laughed. "What do I care? So, Dan is coming. He won't even see me," I said, although I knew this was untrue.

"Of course," cried Almaz, laughing. "Dan always comes to look at you, wondering when he will take you away!"

I reached for Almaz, to give her a swat. She jumped, like a butterfly, still such a little child at nine. Almaz has always been thin and small, and we have let her fly away so. Auntie and I have to catch her to make her do chores.

When I was her age I went down the mountain to the government school. My Aunt Kibret always shook her head about me, because what does a girl need with books? My Aunt Kibret is like a willow in the wind, you see. She speaks in a rush, then changes to the other side. Finally she let me have my way about school but always was afraid the other women would say something.

After what happened to my friend Gennet, and me, I stopped going to school. Our little village is too small for a school, so Almaz was growing up ignorant altogether, and too playful.

When I heard about Dan I went into our *tukel*, because he ought not to see me alone.

Almaz rushed after me. "He has come to tell us about the dream, you know. Weizero Channa has had another dream!"

"How do you know this, little one?"

7

"Everyone knows," Almaz said.

True, in the Simien Mountains news blows like seeds in the wind. We had already heard that Weizero Channa, Dan's grandmother, had had a marvelous dream. She told it first to her son, Kess Haim, the village priest. Now her grandson, Dan was bringing it to us. They live in our next nearest village, a whole day's walk away.

Now, when an ordinary woman has a dream, it is one thing. But when the dream belongs to a very old woman and the mother of a priest, well, that is something else. She had had dreams before that came true. Richly interwoven with many meanings, as the cloth of a holiday *shamma* is interwoven with bright colors, so were Weizero Channa's dreams.

The elders and the little children hurried to meet him. Dan spoke first to our *kess*, Dawit, as is only proper. He bowed to the elders, the wise ones, the weaver, and my uncle Tekle. At last he came near our *tukel*, stood outside.

Dan is very formal and proper. The youngest son of Kess Haim, he has always had to be the silent one, waiting. He waited now. I watched him from the doorway. When my aunt came out to meet him, Dan bowed and kissed her hand, bending his head low. He inquired about everybody's health, at last asking about me. "How is your niece, Desta?" I was listening from within, peering at him standing there in the bright sunlight.

"You may see her for yourself," said Aunt Kibret, smiling. "Desta!" she called, as if I didn't know, "Dan is here."

Dan is tall and slim, like all our men, and his skin is very dark, gleaming like ebony.

He greeted me. "Good day, Desta."

"Hello, Dan," I replied, keeping my head down. Dan is older than I. I don't know how much. We don't bother with birthdays the way white people do.

"I have news," Dan said. "I bring a tale, a dream."

Aunt Kibret invited him into the *tukel* with a clucking, fussing sound. "Come out of the hot sun, Dan! Sit down. Here on the ledge. You must have some *tella*. Desta has brewed it herself, and it is delicious."

I smiled to myself, that my auntie would praise me so, and I got the jug that holds the beer we make from barley and the bitter *gesho* leaves, which I had gathered myself and prepared.

I poured the *tella* to nearly overflowing, so that Dan wouldn't think we give unwillingly.

They talked. How is your father, Kess Haim? And your uncle? How is Weizero Channa? And your father's mule? And your chickens? And how is the harvest over there?

"Very well, very well, thanks to God."

At last my aunt glanced at me, saying, "We are just eating *mett* and *injera*. You must join us."

"No, no Weizero Kibret, I couldn't eat a thing," said Dan, shaking his head. "I am not hungry. Truly, I am filled to bursting."

Aunt Kibret played her part well, pouting, her hands on her hips. "What? You insult me in my own home! You have spoiled my day. My neighbors will think me stingy. You must eat, Dan, I say it!"

Outside the stew was ready and warming on the coals; my mouth watered for the hot spicy sauce, but I knew I would not get even a taste. Three times my aunt would offer. Three times Dan would refuse, or knowing him, he might even refuse an extra time before he gave in.

"Dan, please eat, please" my aunt begged. "Am I not cooking well enough for you? Please try it and tell me—plenty of pepper in it. Turnips, carrots, a bit of chicken, plenty of pepper!" She smiled broadly, her teeth very white against the blackness of her skin, especially in the hut where it was dark.

At last it was settled, and we went outside. I brought the straw table out with us, and Aunt Kibret led Dan to the low tree trunk that makes a seat. We had four pieces of *injera* stored inside the hollow table. I hoped Dan was not too hungry. Food, for us, was always a blessing, and never too plenty. The landlords always take a share, even though they are not supposed to do it anymore. When the Dergue came they said there would be free land for all—ha!

Dan sat down, so correct. I thought, everything he does is just like his father, the *kess*. And I wondered, is there anything of Dan that is himself? Old clucking hen! my aunt Kibret would scold me, for I have thoughts like no other girl, no other proper one, says she.

I could see the beginning of a beard on Dan's cheeks, and I wondered how he would look when it grew full. Dan's eyebrows are heavy, and his eyes, set deep, carry some sorrow. For the rest of my life, I thought, with a feeling like faintness, I would be serving him food just this way. And would he ever look at me? Would he ever laugh? I spooned the *wett* into the *injera*, filling the dough generously. Nobody must ever say that we give poorly.

Dan ate. After each bite he wiped his lips with the edge of his *shamma*. He glanced at me out of the corner of his eye. I added more pepper. Then he actually smiled, making my heart jump. I did not know how to feel about Dan. I was frightened. Dan seemed much too old for me. Too stern. Even my older brother, Joas, laughed more and still knew how to play. Well, this comes from having a priest for a father, I thought. Kess Haim is a very wise man, a known man. He learned Hebrew at a special school in Addis Ababa when he was young. He used to teach boys from our village, Joas among them. Times like this, I wished for my mother. She might have told me about feelings, about men and women and such things as I would soon need to know. Aunt Kibret said I was fortunate. How many girls would give anything to be in my place? Betrothed to the son of a *kess!* Our parents had betrothed Dan and me years ago, when I was still a little child, younger than Almaz.

Dan swayed slightly as old men do when they are about to speak. At last he began. A few children wandered over to listen, and some grownups, too, also Joas my brother.

Dan made a low, murmuring sound deep in his throat. Then he told us the dream, as though he himself had been the dreamer, making it seem even more real.

"Ah, the mountains are so beautiful in the moonlight!" he began, setting the scene like an actor in a play. "The mountains are streaked with color, and the sky is full of stars. Stars in a dream, you know, mean a stranger is coming with gifts, plenty."

Dan paused. He looked at me swiftly. I lowered my eyes, flushed with the look. Did he think me pretty?

Dan continued, his voice trembling slightly. "On the narrow trail a ram appears; its hide gleams milky white in the moonlight. Its noble head is large, showing the greatness of its wisdom, and it has powerful, twisted horns. The ram runs down the mountain, faster and faster across the plain and to a cave, deep and wide. And now a flock of lambs comes following, crowding and bleating, and the ram leads them into the wide mouth of the cave."

I stole a look at Aunt Kibret. She sat transfixed, her hand over her mouth, her eyes very wide, very white. I thought of the saying we have heard so many times from the Bible, of our ancient Queen of Sheba who said the words, "I am black, but comely." My aunt is still comely, her head set proud upon her slim neck, her cheekbones high and beautiful.

Dan continued. "Into the cave the animals crowd, bleating and pushing, and then there is silence as they see before them a vast table covered with pure white linen, and upon the table—" he breathed deep, "candlesticks of gold, and dishes of gold and silver filled with food, with meat and with stew, with breads piled high, ah, with lentils and peas, onion, potato and hot spices, plenty."

My stomach churned. I had not eaten much that day.

"What a beautiful dream!" exclaimed my aunt, and I knew her stomach, too, was roaring with hunger.

"Chicken and honey, beans and barley," continued Dan without mercy, lost in the telling of his grandmother's dream.

"What does it mean?" cried Aunt Kibret, inhaling deeply, leaning toward Dan, to be part of the beautiful dream.

"My grandmother, Weizero Channa," said Dan with a nod all around, "says the dream is very clear. The ram represents our God. He is calling us, His flock, to follow Him. He will lead us out to a land of plenty."

"What land, Dan?" Uncle Tekle came near, dragging his lame leg behind him.

"My grandmother, Weizero Channa, says the days of the return are approaching. There are white Jews in Israel, saying we can come to them. We can come home. Weizero says we will have visitors, too. From far away."

Yagob the other blacksmith, glanced about. "Be careful what you say, boy. The *shum* has big ears, don't you know?"

"Dan, it is dangerous to leave these mountains," said Uncle Tekle, his voice low. "Some have tried." He shook his head.

Dan replied, "My father, Kess Haim, says that the Lord will help us. The way he led the Jews out of Egypt in the old days."

I looked at my brother Joas. His eyes burned, as with fever. "You think the Word is coming true? The promise? Now, in our own time? *Now?*"

Dan nodded. "I believe my grandmother. She is very old. And gifted."

"When does your grandmother say these mysterious strangers will arrive?" asked my aunt. She sounded doubtful but still ready to believe, so that later she might remember it either way: Oh, I knew it was just a wild thought—or yes, yes, I knew Dan spoke the truth, it was an omen, and I knew it all along.

"Soon," said Dan, rising, his *shamma* falling softly around him.

*   *   *

We had been hearing rumors. Jews leaving Ethiopia, a few at a time, walking far, far, then getting to the land promised in the Bible. Zion. Israel. Every day of our lives we have prayed that we might someday return to Jerusalem. But a prayer is one thing, reality another.

That night in our *tukel* it began—the talk, talk, talk.

"Why does he come so far just to tell us a dream?" asked my uncle. "We have heard of people leaving. Also of being caught and tortured. Do we need an old woman's dream to know these things?"

"He comes to see Desta," said my aunt. "That is very clear."

"I don't want him to see me!" I cried.

"Don't raise your voice that way, ever," scolded Kibret. She turned to my uncle. "This is what comes from letting her go to school. A young girl needs a husband," Aunt Kibret muttered, "to teach her some manners, for sure."

I held my tongue. Later, lying on our straw mat with Almaz beside me, I wept softly.

"What is it, Desta?" my little sister whispered. She put her small hand in mine.

"Nothing," I murmured. Then, "I think of Gennet. I miss her."

"You have me," Almaz whispered.

"I have not heard anything about Gennet for too long."

"Maybe the strangers will have news," said Almaz. "The ones Weizero Channa dreamed about."

"Old Weizero dreams too much," I said crossly. I knew old Weizero Channa. She could be wise and fine, or she could be shrill. Even Kess Haim became a little boy again before her sharp tongue. But it was also true she was a good dreamer. Maybe Almaz was right; I longed to hear from Gennet again.

When Gennet and I went to school, we used to take her younger brother, Mare, when he could be spared from the fields. In growing season little boys are needed to guard the crops against birds and wild animals.

At school we did not tell them we were Beta Yisrael. But they found out. Little things. For one thing, we would not eat with them. We follow the laws of Torah; they are very strict about food.

One day there was cholera in the town. Some people died, and everyone was scared, plenty. People asked each other—how did this cholera come to us? Who did it? Someone remembered seeing a Jew in the town; Jews bring the evil eye, don't you know? They can turn themselves into hyenas at night and suck away people's breath. Especially feared is the blacksmith, with his fire. They call him Evil Eye. *Buda*.

Well it happened after school, one of the bigger boys saw Gennet and Mare and me on the road. *"Buda!"* screamed the boy, pointing his finger. "I have seen her with her uncle in the village of S——! He is a blacksmith. They are Falasha!"

A cry went up. "Falasha! Falasha!"

How my heart pounded. I looked for help, stood alone with Gennet and the little brother, my legs shaking.

They came toward us. Gennet tried to hold Mare back, but he bolted. They made a game of it, grabbing Mare's shirt, letting him break free, catching him again, until the little boy was like an animal caught in trap and his eyes large with fright.

They encircled us, tight, screaming, "Falasha! Dirty, dirty Falasha! Killed our Christ. Killing our babies, bringing sickness, poisoning the water, zah! Zah! Zah!"

"Stop it!" I screamed. "Stop it!"

My voice was lost in the roar. They had caught little Mare, and they held him upside down, shaking him, and then as the others held Gennet and me, they beat him with sticks on the soles of his bare feet. It is the usual torture for prisoners; the children had learned it from their parents. Inside I screamed and screamed, but I bit my lip until the blood ran, not to let them hear me.

At last they let him go. We carried little Mare home, and he did not speak or even cry, just lay with his head back against our shoulders, eyes rolling.

After that we did not go back to school. I stayed home and helped Auntie with the pots. Mare could not walk for a long time. His feet swelled triple their size. Gennet changed, too. Her parents had a Christian woman come and tattoo a cross into the middle of her forehead, to try to keep her safe on the roads and in town. They moved to Gondar after that, and I have not seen Gennet since, waiting every day for news.

So I hoped for the truth of Weizero Channa's dream, and that strangers would really come bringing news from Gondar, telling about Gennet.

Well, the very next day, who comes shouting to me, but Almaz, again, *"Sille! Sille!* Hurrah! Desta, Desta, stop the grinding for once and come. Come! It's strangers on the road, just like Weizero said, and mules, Desta, with bundles, plenty!"

"Is it true, Almaz? Look, if you are playing a game, I will punish you, plenty." I looked at her close.

"The boys have seen them from the roof. They have mules and a guide and," she put her hand over her mouth, "Desta, the *shum* is with them too, and he has a gun."

2

ALMAZ AND I HURRIED TO JOIN THE GATHERING CROWD. EVEN Kess Dawit, our priest, looked excited. He beat his walking stick impatiently on the ground.

Dust clouded our vision, but from the size of the spiral we could see it was several donkeys, maybe a string of five or six, making their way up the road. We have few travelers from outside these mountains. Always it is something to be remembered and told for years. This time, of course, the excitement was double, because of Weizero Channa's dream.

As we waited our voices clattered so, filling the space between us, as if we all stood wrapped together in a single garment. What news? Who are they? Why are they here?

We could make out six people, three riding, three walking, one with a rifle, dressed all in gray. That was the *shum*, the official from the Peasants' Association. Such men come to spy on us. If they report us, say we are disloyal, there is trouble, plenty.

Nearly everyone was gathered now, my aunt and uncle

and Joas, too, the elders out front, the *kess* holding his Bible. Silence overtook us as they approached. We Ethiopians always need a space of silence when feelings are strong.

First came the guide in a red shirt and the jeans worn by foreigners and big people in town. You could see that this guide thought himself plenty big, with his red shirt and the way he walked, all shoulders, waving his arms like a *shmagile*, a wise one.

Behind this big one came two donkeys packed with water jugs and strange parcels. Almaz squeezed my arm. Gifts! My heart beat fast—but what of the *shum* with the gun?

This one came next, dressed in Peasant Association gray and that rifle slung over his shoulder. His eyes roved, searching the shadows, and his brows rose to a quick point above them. A narrow nose he had, and high-bridged; we do not trust noses like that. But after the *shum* and the guide another man hurried, almost running toward us there under the acacia tree, where Kess Dawit stood sober and tall, with his *shamma* in dignified folds about him.

"Greetings!" cried the stranger. He spoke in our own tongue. He extended his hands in the African way, bowed to the *kess*, and called out once more, "Greetings, joyous greetings!"

He wore a *shamma* draped over his shoulders, as if to prove that he was still African. But he wore a suit, a real suit, like none we had ever seen. Even more than his clothes, something in his face spoke of other worlds. He had seen wonders. He stood in the midst of the circle we formed around him, and he began to speak to us loudly and with great feeling.

"Joyous greetings! God be with you! We have come to

see you, and bringing gifts. Some of you may remember me,"
continued the stranger. "Or at least you may remember my
name. I am Petros, the son of Yohannes, from the village of
W——, at the other side of the mountain and near the city
of Gondar. And I have brought visitors from far away, very
far."

Even as Petros spoke the three mules lumbered up into
the clearing, all with their riders sitting so stiff, then dismount-
ing, and I say it: They were white. Two men and a woman,
white as anything. *Yeiiii!* Some babies screamed at the sight
of these white faces. One little boy ran howling back to the
tukels, and mothers had to pat their children to quiet them.
I felt Almaz tremble, and I hugged her close. My own heart
was leaping. We had never seen a white person before.

The guide began to swagger: "There is not much to
see here," he said, with a glance at the *shum.* "These are
only poor farmers with nothing to sell."

Petros gazed at our *kess,* murmuring, "I bring brethren.
From far away," said Petros. "From America. They wanted
to see you."

America? We knew the word, but had no idea of the
distance. Why would a person come from America to us, to
the Simien mountains, and on the back of a mule?

Kess Dawit stood ramrod straight, his eyes roving to the
guide, to the strangers, to Petros. "To see us? Why?"

Words flew, rattling from the woman, onto Petros, who
translated.

"You are Jews, aren't you? Beta Yisrael?" came the woman's words. "We have come so far to see you, surprised to
learn that you live here so high in these mountains. We never

knew there were black Jews in the world—so we came to see you, bringing gifts. We want you to know it: You are not alone."

Old Fanta, Gola's mother, fell to her knees and gave out a shrill cry of joy. "Liiliiiliiii!" I guess she thought it was the Messiah.

More talk, questions and questions, coming through Petros, talking fast, nervous, but giving out the words just the same. The white ones must have paid him plenty for the risk he took.

"How long have you lived here?"

"Our fathers' fathers are buried here."

"Have you had visitors before?"

"A few. Long ago. We wrote their names in a book."

"We have read about other visitors coming here. Do you know the name Jacques Faitlovich?" asked the older white man.

"Our fathers knew him. He was a good man. He brought news and books. He taught our people. . . . He was a good man."

"We have read about him, and about you," the white woman exclaimed. "I wanted to see you! Falashas."

At that word a flicker came into Kess Dawit's eyes, and he grasped his staff tighter. "We have few visitors," he said. "We are simple people. We obey the law."

"Do you know about Israel?"

"Where is that? In this country?"

"Don't you know that Israel is the land belonging to the Jewish people?"

"They are ignorant," said the guide with contempt.

"They do not know much, only how to make trouble."

"What is their work?" asked the white ones. "Are they farmers? Do they own land? Are they treated fairly?"

The guide spoke, his eyes flashing toward the *shum.* "Of course they can own land," he said loudly. "Everyone is equal here. The revolution has brought freedom and fairness to all."

Kess Dawit gazed off to the distance. "We are simple people," he said. "We live as we have always lived, and like our fathers' fathers before us."

"But aren't you Jews? Are you free to learn Torah?"

Kess Dawit raised himself up. He sighed. "We live," he said. "We are like the people in ancient Babylon. You know the words? They hanged their harps on the willow tree . . ."

Ah, now there was silence indeed as these words took hold, and tears in the eyes of the white woman, the white men nodding sorrowfully; they understood. In the days of the Bible, some Jews were taken captive to Babylon. They would not sing for their captors, but wept for Jerusalem, longing for home. Just so, we were captives here in Ethiopia.

"That is the Old Testament," said the *shum.* He swung his rifle around. "Nobody believes in this nonsense anymore. We have tried to tell them it is a bad habit keeping the old ways. These people are Ethiopians, like all of us."

"These people complain too much," said the guide. "They speak falsely about our Glorious Revolution. You see, they have this book which gives them evil commands."

"Their Bible?" The older white man reached out his hand. "May we see your Bible?"

22

The Kess looked beyond the *shum*. He could no longer remain silent. "In the past, many people came to convert us. They said we were the only Jews left in the world. It was not true. But we said, even if we are the only ones, we still keep the commandments. We do not deny our God. Even if they kill us." Silently Kess Dawit brought forth his book, wrapped in string, for the pages are old and brittle.

"Is this the Torah?" asked the white man, his eyes gentle, longing.

Kess Dawit nodded. "We are people of the Torah. Yes, we are. We follow the commandments."

"We too are people of the Torah," said the woman, whispering. "We have the same history, the same longing."

Zion. What else is the longing of a Jew? Zion.

"I have been to Jerusalem," said Petros now, using the Hebrew word, *"Yerushalayim."*

I cannot fully describe the effect of this word, Jerusalem, upon all of us there in the clearing. Almaz, still clinging to my hand, leapt up once, shrill with excitement, and I clapped my hand over her mouth. I looked at Petros's feet, to see the shoes that have walked that holy city. My hands felt numb, my mind dizzy. Jerusalem. Was it really a true place? I looked for Joas. His eyes blazed.

"Would you let us see your Bible up close?" they asked. "Would you let us see your holy relics? Will you show us the house where you live?"

For an Ethiopian to deny a visitor hospitality is impossible. And the *shum* and guide would never enter a Falasha dwelling, afraid of the Evil Eye.

"Yes, yes," cried Kess Dawit. "Of course, you must

come to my *tukel*. Yes, yes, you must eat and drink with us." He glanced at the *shum*, for the first time smiling. "It is the Ethiopian way."

The *shum* dragged his feet. A look was given; several of the elders went to distract the *shum*, bringing the younger white man along. "Come, come down to the river and cool your feet. You must be thirsty, plenty, after this climb. This young man wants to see the fields and the pottery and the iron work, isn't it so?"

"Yes, yes. We'll show him everything."

Kess Dawit led the way, to his *tukel*, the largest in the village. I could see that he was troubled, and he muttered his thoughts to those near him.

"This has been foretold," he said, "but others have come here posing as Jews, trying to convert us. Some have offered to lead us to Zion, only to steal our few possessions, to sell us into slavery, or lead us into the hands of bandits. . . ."

"These are good people," said Petros. "You will see."

Many people crowded into the *tukel*, and it was hot, too. The white people stared. Petros kept wiping his forehead with his *shamma*. I guess he'd been gone so long he forgot what it is to be tight in a *tukel* with all your kin and even a few goats tagging along with their own smell.

Of course the *kess*'s wife brought the coffee, and sat to grind it fine, with everyone around watching, and, oh, she was proud! At last it was done, and the visitors drank it, the white woman looking strange, her eyes closed.

The children were getting restless, and all were aware of the guide standing outside the *tukel*, as far from its shadow as he could go without looking too scared.

24

Well, it had to be proved. They looked at our books.
"What passage are you reading in the Torah this week?"
The Kess told it.

"We are reading the same in our congregation in New
York!"

Now, tears and smiles all together, hands holding hands,
black and white; now they knew each other as brethren,
truly, and could cry together. It was so beautiful, but the
little children like Almaz started to itch and scratch.

Joas came to stand with us and held Almaz's shoulders
to keep her still. I could hear his swift breathing. My brother
wears an old military coat with two brass buttons, and I thought
how splendid he would look in a real uniform, or even in a
suit. He is very handsome, my brother, really the best-looking
boy in our village.

The white woman spoke. Then Petros looked around,
and he asked the question, "Can anyone here speak Hebrew?
The visitors would like to hear."

Hebrew? A few of the boys have learned a little, and
long ago. Kess Dawit knows no Hebrew; our holy books are
written in Geez.

Nobody moved. I felt that strange leaping in my chest,
as if I knew already what was coming, and then beside me
Joas found his voice and called out strongly, "I do."

Quickly hands reached out to Joas, to push him up to
the *kess* and the others, and from his pocket Joas took the
battered primer he always carries with him, not because he
is so holy, but because it is his possession, you see.

A small oil lamp was brought from the niche, held close,
with the elders looking on, nodding as if they also could

read the words. My brother Joas bent his head to the book, and he called out, "Shema Yisrael Adonay Elohaynu Adonay echad," and other Hebrew words, too. Now they wept truly—I think old people like to cry the way we children like to laugh.

After the weeping, time for the presents at last. Petros had brought a large blue bag. Across its top, like a silver streak, something glittered and suddenly—zup!—flew apart, showing many things. Petros pulled the thing once again, so that it locked itself tight into place. With another tug, the bag was laid open again. "It is called a zipper," Petros said proudly.

"Ha!" The *kess* strode forward and tried it himself with his old hands and was pleased to make it close again. "So, this is what they make in Jerusalem." He used the old remembered word, Yerushalayim." He turned to us. "You see, in Yerushalayim marvelous things appear, with only the turn of a wrist."

Out of the bag did come wonderful things—matches in small boxes, paper, stout cord and string and embroidery thread of different colors, and I heard Aunt Kibret gasp.

There were sewing needles and soap and metal spoons and knives, and red tablets to give strength to children, and bottles of pink medicine to use against worms.

And then Petros took out the books.

A hush fell over the group in the *tukel*. The *kess*'s eyes went cloudy with tears.

"I will leave these books with you," Petros said. "They are Passover Haggadoth from Israel."

Petros read from the book. The words were strange,

but the rhythm was somehow familiar. Then he said, "These prayers are written in Hebrew, but they are exactly the same as yours." He translated into our language, Amharic. "Why is this night different from all other nights . . ?"

Beside me I heard Joas breathe, "It's the same. Exactly the same."

Petros continued. "And I have brought you something else. Very special. From our white brothers and sisters, with love."

Now Petros took out a large box. "Matzos," Petros said. "For the Passover. This is square, you see, while yours is round, but it is the same unleavened bread which we eat to celebrate the exodus of the Jews from Egypt."

Of course we make matzos every year. It was incredible for me to imagine that white people somewhere across the sea shared our Passover, and sent us these matzos in a box.

They were indeed brethren. Now we could tell them the truth about our lives. The men talked and talked, telling it all, and the white ones nodded and sighed at how we have suffered.

"The Dergue, the hellish Dergue!" my uncle said bitterly. "And they tell us everything is equal now! Land reform?" He gave a bitter laugh. "What reform? We still pay and pay—if not to the government, then to our neighbors."

The men explained it: Yes, the new government said we could own land now, and the Peasants' Association was supposed to see that we got our share. But other tribes still took the best plots for themselves, and what little was left to us was rocky and steep. The neighbors still demanded rent. If we did not pay they broke our *tukels* and beat our men senseless. They beat Uncle Tekle so badly that he is lame.

The men groaned as they told it: "They changed market day to our Sabbath, so now we must hire a Muslim to take our wares to market for us, and paying plenty for it. But that is not the worst. They won't let us study. They torture our teachers, close our schools. Our children grow up ignorant, like mules, like savages without Torah."

Softly the *kess* said, "Of course we know about Israel. But who has the money to go there? And even if we had the means, the government will not let us leave. Those who try to go are arrested. Sometimes the *shum* comes to count the villagers. If some Jews have escaped, they punish those remaining."

"We wish we could help you," murmured the white ones. Of course, they could not.

I looked at the white woman. Her flesh was soft and gathered well upon her body. Her hair was straight and shone with silvery streaks. Her skin was marked with tiny spots, like the shell of a bird's egg; her eyes were like the sky, and her face creased with some age and wisdom starting to show there, and beautiful.

She caught me looking, smiled.

More than anything in the world I wanted to smile back at her, to touch her skin, to ask a question, one question of the thousands that beat in my brain like grasshoppers fluttering wild—where is America? How many Jews live there? Do they go to school? Do they trade with Christians? What is that gold in your tooth? A treasure? And what are those glass ornaments before your eyes—do they have to do with Torah, keeping the commandments?

28

I could only stare, seeing the faint light hairs on her arms, the garments she wore, pants like a man, and a jacket with buttons of brass shining so. She wore boots with laces. She was rich, you could see it, yet no bracelets or earrings or necklaces shone on her, only a plain ring of gold.

Before I could think, Almaz darted away, touched the woman's arm with her fingers, smiling, ah! "Weizero, Weizero!" Almaz chirped in her little girl way, "How I love you!"

The woman was startled, then bending, gathered Almaz close, held her there to her softness and cried out in words I did not understand, "What a beautiful child!" and Petros said them to us out loud in Amharic, "What a beautiful child!"

I wanted to hide. I wanted also to take that touch, to be held. I hung my head, bit my lip, choking down the sudden bitter anger at Almaz. I was glad to see Aunt Kibret giving Almaz a look, scolding her without words. Almaz, like a little angel, only smiled back. I pinched her.

Now the woman brought out a box, black and small. Petros explained it. She wanted to keep the sight of our Torah.

Keep it? We turned our heads, wondering.

Suddenly a small bit of lightning flashed.

Zing! A grinding. Paper rolled out. And then, even as we watched, crowding close, some colors did come to that paper, and shapes, too, and then before us it was clear: a tiny Kess Dawit standing tall, holding the Torah in his arms.

"Polaroid," said Petros. "This is how they keep memories."

Not one of us could understand it, but we all wished for a memory like this. She did it once again. Zing! and she gave one of the memories to the *kess*, to keep forever, and I guess he still has it tucked into that Bible of his.

Outside, we all crowded around, waving and weeping as the strangers left. "Don't forget us!" we called.

"How could we?" they answered.

They said words in Hebrew. Later Joas told me the meaning: "Peace to you. Peace. Next year in Jerusalem."

The ancient blessing, now come alive.

I looked over at my Aunt Kibret. "Talk, talk," she said, and she tapped her foot. "Talk is plenty, here, as plentiful as our troubles."

Almaz clung to Joas's arm, chattering, "What's it like in Jerusalem, Joas? What do people do all day?"

He scooped her up, laughing. "They do nothing but dance and sing. They walk along the golden streets. Let's go there, little one!"

Almaz laughed, and Aunt Kibret tossed her head, her expression sour. But I caught Joas's look, and I knew what he was thinking.

Almaz sighed. "We'll never go there then. It's heaven."

3

THAT NIGHT AFTER EVENING PRAYERS WHEN EVERYONE WAS asleep, I heard a noise outside, a scratching of two twigs being rubbed together. It was our sign, Joas's and mine. Joas got big, and our *tukel* was small, so Joas slept outside unless it was raining.

I crept outside. The moon was nearly full, with only a small broken edge, like a piece of *injera* with a bite eaten out.

"Desta," Joas whispered.

I squatted down beside him. "What is it? Everyone is asleep."

"While you took Almaz to bathe in the stream this afternoon," he whispered, "I went with the strangers down to the crossroads. We talked."

"You went with them?" I gazed at him, envious. Boys can do anything, I thought.

"I talked to Petros. The guide and the *shum* were busy getting out of these mountains, fast." Joas laughed; he laughs well and often. "Petros told me about Jerusalem. He himself is going back there. He has a visa."

I did not know what a visa was. I was not even certain of Jerusalem. Maybe such a place didn't really exist, but was only mentioned in prayers, like paradise.

"What did he say about Jerusalem?" I challenged. "That there is gold in the streets? That people sing and dance all day?"

"He told me that Jews from many lands live there together. And they are free. Nobody persecutes them. They live in peace. White and black. Some from Morocco, Yemen, Persia."

My head reeled; the moon was spinning around me. What did I know of such places? In school we learned a little about numbers and letters; we recited the dates of the Glorious Revolution and the names of its leaders. But I had never traveled farther than to the market at T——. How could I imagine Jerusalem, much less Morocco, Yemen, and Persia?

"So they live there," I said, my lip thrust out. "Good for them."

"We can go too," Joas said. He gazed at me. "Let's do it, Desta. We can do it. Desta, don't you understand what it would mean to live in Israel? We could breathe. . . . we could even pray out loud."

"It is not so terrible here, Joas," I said.

"Let's go, Desta. You are a good walker. And strong. We can do it."

"What about Almaz?"

"Give her extra food," Joas said. "She is too thin, for

sure. Let her get fatter before the journey."

"Almaz can't be stuffed like a fowl," I retorted. "You are crazy, Joas."

"Desta, why won't you trust me?"

"I trust you plenty. The best is, to trust oneself."

"I wouldn't let anything happen to you, Desta. Look, in Jerusalem you can go to school. You can learn pottery, even."

"I don't know pottery? I am a fine potter. Everyone says so."

"You could get paid for it. Not like here, only a fraction of the value of your work, because you are a Falasha and they take advantage."

I held my breath. "It is too dangerous, Joas."

"Others have done it."

"Auntie told you! If Dergue soldiers catch people on the road they are tortured. Maybe killed. Didn't you hear? One of the elders from the village of D—— was caught on the road. They broke his legs. He won't walk again. His daughter was with him. The guards did things to her. . . . you know." I moistened my lips, turned away from him. "What men can do to women." Such things are not spoken of between brother and sister.

Joas grunted. "We must try, Desta. If I stay here, the Dergue will get me, and if they don't, there are the others. The People's party. Or the Revolutionary committee. They all want boys for their armies. They have come to other villages. They will come here too."

"Look, Joas," I said, "we are high in the mountains. They don't come here looking for soldiers."

"Oh, no? Didn't you see the *shum* just today? With the rifle? How he looked at me? They have their quota to bring to the army. I say it!"

"Stop shouting at me!" I cried, and clapped my hands over my ears, though in truth Joas wasn't shouting at all, but whispering angrily.

"What a coward you are," he scorned. "What a little coward."

"This is useless talk," I said, turning as if to leave him. But I was held by the moonlight, by my brother's stinging words. *Coward.* "Uncle could never walk to Jerusalem. It is far, isn't it?"

Of course, I already knew he meant to leave them here. I could not think about it yet, or say it.

"Walk to Jerusalem!" Joas threw back his head, laughing. "We wouldn't walk clear to Jerusalem, you old hen! Look, we would walk to Sudan. It's not too far."

"How far?"

"Two weeks."

"Ha!" I knew something about our neighboring countries; I am not ignorant altogether.

"Three weeks, then," Joas agreed. "So, we can walk for three weeks. By night. In the daytime we rest. There are guides."

"They'll take us for free?" I stood up and crossed my arms over my chest, the way Kibret does when she argues.

"Not for free," said Joas.

Deeply I breathed in the night air to steady myself. I made my voice light, almost teasing. "So now, smart brother of mine, what about the money?"

"I figured you will save a little from your pottery, and I will save a little from my metalwork and maybe work extra on the Amhara farms at harvest time for cash."

"It would take a year."

"Better start now, then," Joas said, jaw firm. "Desta, listen, we suffer here. You don't even know what it is to be free. Wouldn't you like to go to school? To read books? To be able to walk on the roads without hiding whenever you hear a noise? Everything that happens in Ethiopia they blame on us—sickness, bad crops, drought, and famine. Can't you see what is happening? What about your friend Gennet, with a cross burned into her flesh. Is this how you want to live?"

"Don't talk to me about Gennet!"

"It is always Falasha! Falasha! I'm sick of it!"

"How can you think of leaving our uncle and aunt?" I cried. "Without us, who would help uncle at the forge? Who would help Aunt Kibret make the pots to sell for money? They have cared for us like their own. And what about Almaz?"

"Oh, why do I bother talking to you?"

"Because we are *zamed*."

His voice changed, flowing. "That is why I don't want to go without you. Desta, don't make me choose between my blood kin and Jerusalem."

"You are making me choose!" I cried.

"Brothers and sisters are closer than uncle and aunt," he argued, growing angry. "Besides," he said, "it is written. In the Bible. Jerusalem is our real home. Would you say no to God?"

I trembled with rage. I thought, without speaking the words, how dare you? How dare you bring God's name into this, to make me afraid? To force me to do your bidding?

Suddenly I was overcome, and I sat with knees clutched tight to my chest, weeping. Joas touched my shoulder. I felt the heat from his hand.

"Go away!" I pushed him. "Go dream out there with the moon!"

I heard the rustling of his footsteps, and I peered up to see his dark form retreating over to a clump of bushes, and then he was out of sight.

It was some weeks later, and I was in the women's hut, having just come down with the monthly curse. When she brought me my supper, Aunt Kibret was full of news. Guess who came to the village today? Who else but Kess Haim and Dan. And there was talk about me.

I was glad to be in the women's hut. I did not want to hear it. For two winters now I have been coming each month to the *Margam Bet*, the House of Blood. It is pleasant for women to be together. We can wander about the village, but we are not allowed to work or touch food, so our kinswomen come to feed us. Often the Margam Bet is filled with laughter. Women alone together laugh plenty, mostly about men.

With me this time was Alemu, a young mother who had just given birth to a daughter. Mother and child were blissful. While the baby suckled, Alemu and I talked and talked. We took turns rubbing the tiny infant with oil. Her skin was so soft under my fingertips! I felt strange sensations in my breasts and in my belly. I envied Alemu the sweet brown baby at her breast, and yet I did not want to get married.

We sat outside on straw mats in the coolness of afternoon, talking and laughing. "Marriage is not so bad," Alemu said. "Men are difficult, for true, but they can also give pleasure. And then there are babies. Like this fat little one. You would be married already, Desta," said Alemu, "if it weren't for the troubles around us, war and revolution."

"Girls don't always marry so young anymore," I reminded her. "Things are changing. Almaz isn't even betrothed."

"That is true," said Alemu with a distant look. "I hear your brother speak about Jerusalem. Taking you and Almaz."

"You hear him?"

"Everyone knows Joas would be the first to go." Alemu laughed. "He has always been the adventurer. If you go to Israel," said Alemu, "you would not have to marry Dan, isn't it so?"

I stared at Alemu, my heart leaping to my mouth. Just then I heard Auntie's voice as she came up the hill to the hut with my basket of food and water. She was breathless from the climb.

"Desta! Sweet one!" She greeted Alemu, too, with smiles and kisses, plenty. "Alemu, how goes it today? And how is that fine fat baby? A blessing. A joy. The Lord smiled on you, Alemu."

Auntie must have seen something strange on my face, for she peered at me, asking, "What is the matter with you?"

"Nothing, nothing," I said, with a hand pressed to my middle. "Only the usual."

"There has been talk about you," Aunt Kibret said, moving aside with me to give Alemu some rest. "Dan's father spoke with your Uncle Tekle for a long time this morning.

37

Kess Dawit was there, too. Dan's father wants a wedding before the big harvest ends. It is time for his son to plant a crop." Aunt Kibret gave me a look, steady and stern. "He does not mean *teff* or corn."

My cheeks burned. Who speaks of such things? Sullenly I said, "So, you want to be rid of me, isn't it so?"

"Desta, for shame." My aunt shook herself, flapping like a chicken, nervous. "You are going to be an old virgin forever, with nobody to look after you, dependent on your brother, and everyone will say it was my fault, that I did not get you married, that I went against the wishes of your parents."

The thought drummed in me—Alemu's words. If I went to Israel I would not have to marry Dan. "Don't worry for me, Auntie!" my tone was sharp. "You'll get rid of me soon enough!"

"Desta, for shame!"

We heard a call. "*Sille!* Little mother, dear one, how goes?" It was Mehret, the midwife, Alemu's kinswoman coming to bring her food, her voice preceding her. "*Sille! Sille!*" she called gaily, laughing, and the bundles quivered on her back. "How is the new mother? Ah, lovely one, yes, bring the child out into the air. Take a cool breath, my dear. I brought you fresh *injera* and *tella* just settled; the beer increases mother's milk, eh?"

The two women kissed again and again, cheek to cheek, and then we all exchanged greetings and kisses, the way we do.

My aunt said, "Congratulations on this fine fat baby, though it is a girl."

"Many thanks, many thanks," said Mehret. She always carries a bright purple parasol, and now she twirled it round, so. "Well, we cannot make sons only," she said, laughing. "Girls have their value, if quarrelsome they may be."

"Quite true," said my Aunt Kibret faintly, and I knew she was thinking we had been overheard. Her features tightened and she pulled me over behind the hut.

"You cannot behave like a child forever," she said, her lips firm, eyes flashing. "What can we tell Dan's father?"

"Tell him . . ." I turned away. Angry words had rushed into my mouth; I bit them back.

"Desta!" My aunt grasped my shoulders. "Do you hate him so much, then?"

"No! How can I hate him?" I cried, trying to control myself. "I hardly know him."

"But you see him every year at festivals," my aunt chided, brushing my cheeks with her long fingers. "You know his family, you have been to his village." She gave me a little shake.

"He is so stern," I whispered. "He hardly looks at me. He never says anything nice to me."

"Why should he say anything? He has taken you already for his betrothed."

"He acts as if he already owns me!" I cried. "Don't you remember the time he and Kess Haim came to our village and saw me making the clay figures? How they said I must not play with clay anymore? That I had to do woman's work?"

"And they were exactly right," my aunt exclaimed.

"There is nothing wrong with making pretty things."

"They wanted you to grow up proper, learning how to

spin and bake and keep a proper household. Desta, Desta, what is the matter with you?"

Suddenly I burst into tears.

"Ah, Desta," Aunt Kibret said now, comforting. "Listen, don't be afraid. He is a gentle person. I see it in his face." Her mouth twitched. "The poor boy, he must be quite mad with the need of you! What do you expect from him? He has been waiting these many years, already a man."

"I'm not afraid," I said stoutly. Auntie saw the lie.

"Desta, all young girls are shy and scared before marriage. It should be so, if the girl is pure."

Suddenly a look of horror crossed her face, so that I leaped back, as if she had slapped me hard. "It is so, isn't it?" she asked, her eyes wide. "You are—you haven't been— Desta? Tell me!"

"You know me better than that. Aunt Kibret, how can you think this? How can you imagine I would be . . . be . . ."

"Hush!" she scolded. "I have a right to know. When you went to A—— that time, weeks ago, did you meet anybody on the road? Did anyone speak to you? Did you stop at a house?"

"*No, Auntie, no.* All of it, no," I said, making my voice soft, but with great effort. My chest heaved, and I felt dizzy, but I forced myself to whisper. "Nobody. Nothing, Aunt Kibret. I swear. I would die before I let any man touch me. I would fight! Auntie, I am only frightened. They say that men . . . well, you know. On the wedding night, the man is like a warrior, so fierce, and the woman must . . ."

"All right. All right," soothed my aunt, relenting and

releasing my arm. "I must go to your uncle, to give him food."

I watched her go, her hips swaying. Again, I thought of Alemu's words. . . . If you go to Israel . . .

My aunt turned back, her features now taut, her tone resolute. "We must do what is right, Desta. I cannot let you shame the whole village. We must give Dan the answer, and it must be yes. Your mother, God rest her soul, and your father, they wanted this for you. How can you deny them their last wish? Think of them, if not of me and your Uncle Tekle. Would you defy the dead?"

First Joas had accused me of denying God, and now Kibret accused me of denying the dead. I had no answer either, except for the ache in my chest and visions of my parents together when I was small.

They loved each other truly. You could see it in the way they walked together on the road. When my father went to the market, he came back with blue glass beads for my mother.

I remember she used to look at him when he spoke, not the way most women do, eyes downcast and lowly. But when they were together in our *tukel*, they looked at each other, full, and in the night I heard the sounds of their breathing and of their love.

I saw him touch her belly when it became round and full, with Almaz inside.

Three days after Mama went to the women's hut, the wailing began. I was still small, but of course I knew what it meant. They brought the baby to my Uncle Tekle, father's brother, and Aunt Kibret had to find a woman to nurse Almaz, for my mother was dead. Soon afterward my father was dead too, from poisons or evil spells, who can say?

Now I was glad for these days away from the rest of them, tucked away in the House of Blood. I did not want to move to Dan's village. I did not want to become the handmaiden of old Weizero Channa. I did not want to see anyone, certainly not Dan, with his talk of crops and plantings!

4

WHO CAN SAY WHAT GOD WANTS US TO DO? JOAS SAID GOD
wants us to live in Jerusalem, that it is written we will go
there. Well, if it is written, why has it taken so long and so
much trouble? And why did He send us to Ethiopia in the
first place?

Maybe to learn some lessons, Joas would say. I don't
know.

Alemu said if I went to Israel I would not have to marry
Dan. So now I was living the days and weeks in confusion.
Is it God's will for me to marry Dan? Or not? How much is
God pushing me this way or that, how much is only in my
head, which Aunt Kibret says is stiff with stubbornness, like
a mule?

I began to have dreams of golden streets with people
walking, dressed in beautiful woven *shammas* and carrying
bright parasols, the women with so many necklaces that they
glittered in the sunlight; the warm streets of the city gave
off a sweetness like blossoms in summer, and people smiled

and kissed in greeting, and babies were laughing always.

My heart yearned for Jerusalem, I say it!

But something else in me twisted like a snake, coiled with fear.

The talk went on, night after night, through the Passover week, into late spring and summer. In his heart, Joas was getting ready, for true. Once I came upon him digging under the shed where we store *teff*. He straightened, stared at me with wide eyes.

"What are you hiding?"

"What do you care? Whatever plans I have, they do not include you, coward."

I knew he was hiding money. For Jerusalem. I wanted to hold his arm and cry out, "Don't go without me, my brother! I'm coming with you."

But I could not say it. The thing flew back and forth in my mind, night and day, day and night. Go. Stay. Go. Then I'd see Aunt Kibret's face or notice how the daisies clung to the hillside and the goats ran stiff legged and bleating on the path—I'd see everything that was sweet and good and familiar, and I'd think, well, this problem will go away.

But it didn't.

As we gathered the clay for our pottery, our friend Simha nodded at Aunt Kibret, making vigorous talk. "They say there is famine in Tigre and Wollo," said Simha. "They will probably blame us for it, as usual." Her eyes were turned down, also her mouth.

"We have lived with their lies before," my aunt retorted, "and we will again."

"Not if we leave," said Simha glancing sideways at Kibret.

"Simha," said my aunt, "We are not even allowed to travel to Gondar without a permit."

"My husband, the *shmagile*, says it is possible now to leave. If one is brave. And strong."

"Good-bye, have a pleasant trip," said Kibret, her hands on her hips, glaring. Furiously Kibret dug out the clay, then hoisted the basket onto her shoulder and began to walk. It was hot. Drought coming to the rest of the country meant only small rains for us here in the hills, which mean hard soil, a small crop, and everyone a little hungrier but, thanks to God, we were better off than many others in Africa, this I know.

Auntie wiped her face, breathing hard. "Joas talks about walking all the way to Sudan. What nonsense! The boy is crazy; always something new to bring me worries. And now you."

"Many people are going to Sudan," said Simha, hurrying to keep up with my angry aunt. "Not only Jews are leaving Ethiopia. Muslims and Christians, too. Getting away from hunger. Getting away from war. Listen, Kibret, my husband the *shmagile* says we can go also. With so many people out on the road, we can lose ourselves among them. Blend in. Maybe this is how God is making the prophecy come true. Don't you see? We are destined for Zion. Don't you know it?"

"Are you a *kess*, that you know our destiny so well?" Aunt Kibret walked even faster. "After two thousand years, why now?"

"Kibret, you are being stormy. I tell you these things I have learned; you have never been one to listen."

We made our way up the incline to our *tukels*, walking slower now from the heat and the heavy baskets, Aunt Kibret puffing from anger as much as from the sun.

"Why would the people of Sudan let us on their land? Simha, does your husband, the *shmagile* say what the people of Sudan want from us in return?" Kibret's tone was sharp.

"Maybe they have plenty of land and don't mind a few more bodies sitting there," said Simha. "There also we can mingle with the others."

My aunt was puffing still as we sat down to knead the clay outside our *tukel*.

"How can we mingle?" She lent her body's weight to her words as she folded the clay and slapped it down, hard. "We look different. Smell different. *Are* different."

She swatted at the chickens pecking the ground for stray bits of grain. "Be gone!"

She broke off a lump of clay, rapidly began to coil, pressing down with her palms. "That Simha is always talking, talking. *Shmagile*, ha! Her man is no more a wise one than this rooster. Bandits in the mountains. Zah! Soldiers on the roads. And she wants to walk to Sudan, to 'mingle'. Almaz," she called. "I want you to churn that yogurt now!"

Almaz took up the gourd and began to churn, singing in a high tone, keeping her own rhythm.

I leaned into the clay the way my aunt had taught me, dreaming of the solution. Yes, maybe we could get Uncle to Gondar or Addis Ababa on a mule or a horse. From there we could take a boat and all go to Israel together. Yes. That was the way it should be, the family together, of course.

"This yogurt is finished," piped up Almaz.

"Then start on the butter," ordered Kibret.

"Joas told me that in Jerusalem nobody has to churn butter or anything," said Almaz, laughing.

Roughly my aunt tore off another hunk of clay and pounded it down. "Look, you!" she shouted. "The Bible says that someone will come to lead us. The Messiah. When the Messiah comes, then we will go to Israel, all together. I don't want to talk about it anymore."

"But Auntie . . ." said Almaz.

"Enough!"

But Joas, coming from the forge, took it up again. He could no more be silent than the owls in the trees could quit their whoo-whooing. "We cannot wait for the government to let us go. You know the army takes the Jewish boys and puts them on the front lines to catch the rebel bullets. Auntie, we have talked much about it before. I'm in danger here!"

"I know," said Kibret. I saw the sweat spread over her face, saw her breathing, deep and hard. "I worry for you. You children are my responsibility."

"You always say we should have faith, Auntie," said Joas.

Kibret put away the pots and scrubbed her hands; I, too. Then she faced Joas, standing tall, hands on her hips. "It takes more than faith to go such distances!"

"There will be planes to take us to Israel. I have spoken to Kess Haim. There are ways to get out of Sudan. Secret ways."

"Such a secret," said Kibret, "pardon me if I laugh, is so well kept that nobody knows it."

Uncle Tekle shuffled over, shaking his head. He dipped

out some water, washed his face and head. Drops of water glistened on his skin. He asked, "Is there coffee?"

"A thin brew only," replied my aunt.

When the rains fail in other regions, we also suffer. Not only because the other tribes blame us. But when their crops fail, they have no money to buy from us, pottery or tools. Then we have less, too, as with coffee, and must rely on our poor crops, grown on the poorest soil. You see, in Africa it is so clear how each tribe is linked to the other, and the bad fortune of one brings misery to all.

Uncle Tekle sat thoughtful, sipping the weak coffee and rubbing his chin. "I can understand Joas. If I were a young man, and strong, I would leave Ethiopia."

I gasped sharply. Until now, Uncle had only listened to Joas day by day, nodding and thinking, stroking his chin.

"You would leave everything? Your kin? Your village?" Kibret exclaimed.

Uncle Tekle frowned deeply, shaking his head. "How must it feel to have a choice?"

"What do you mean?" cried Aunt Kibret, her voice rising. "We have always had the choice. The choice to leave home, maybe die out there in the wilderness? To be robbed or maimed by bandits out in the hills? Me, I would rather lay my head down here in my own *tukel* and in peace. You fill the boy's head with wild ideas. No wonder he is always stormy, restless, roaring."

"Silence, woman!" cried my uncle, "Why don't you tell him the truth? We look to Joas for our old age. We do not want to be left alone."

Aunt Kibret's face changed; it seemed to wither, and

she turned away. It is a heavy burden for a woman to be barren and to remember that she will have nobody to tend her in old age.

I went to her. I put my hand on her shoulder, murmuring low. I wanted to make her a promise. To say it, "I'll never leave you, Aunt Kibret, never!" But it stuck in my throat like a stone.

She did not turn to me, but patted my hand again and again, looking to the distance, as if she already knew something I didn't.

What is it that makes a person see that which was hidden before? Strange, isn't it? Day after day can roll along the same, but suddenly a little hole is worn through a curtain that covers the eyes, the little hole gets bigger, and the world out there no longer looks the same.

It began with the sign of Weizero Channa's dream, then the visit of Petros and the white ones, and then Joas's talking, talking, and gradually I began to see things in new ways. It was true, the coffee was a thin brew, the pot of *wett* more often empty than full. But this was the least of it. You see, I began to notice: Our mouths were always half covered in fear. When strangers came upon us on the road, our hearts raced as if we were guilty. In the night I sometimes awakened, trembling, to realize that it was our own watchman pacing there, and I began to wonder, why should we need protection while we sleep in our own homes? Why?

I thought and I thought: Maybe Joas was right, and Simha, too. With so many people on the roads and soldiers rushing here and there in confusion, with everything changing on the land, maybe we could go and not be noticed. Who would notice a few more people wandering there?

I had expected to see people wandering, their possessions on their backs, when Auntie and I went to T—— for the midweek market. But we saw only the usual. Muslim traders with their carts, a few Amhara peasants bringing produce, and Jews like us, with their iron works or pottery, careful to walk just so, not to give offense to anyone.

The other tribes have a saying: "If a Jew crosses onto our land, the grass will never grow again."

A Muslim family hurried past us. The children stared at me. One little girl covered her face with her hands and peered out, then whispered to her mother, and I heard the word *buda*. I wanted to laugh at her and not care. But that day it hurt me; the little girl looked something like Almaz, gentle and sweet. How could she hate me just at sight, and fear me?

Well, I forgot about it as we walked, our heads high and so proud! It was early, and we were on the way to market, walking on the road with the jars and with our excitement.

Friends stopped us on the road to give greeting, bowing and nodding and sometimes kissing. We were dressed in clean clothes, my hair washed and oiled. Around my neck I wore the blue beads from my mother. Aunt Kibret, with a new white cloth round her head, looked beautiful, for true.

I felt breathless to know that soon I would see the treasures laid out so fine—spices, all kinds of peppers, spoons, cups, beads, household things of new metal, very light, very fine. There was a section for animals, small goats and sheep to be sold for taking home, live, then to slaughter the beast

50

in one's own way. In the big markets people can buy cattle and donkeys and mules. Here in the small market, not many animals, but still it was filled with people, many more than our small village holds.

In the market they always said that Aunt Kibret's water jugs were the best. Even the Amharas said it as they snapped their fingernails against the pottery, testing the ring of it. We sold two jars and three large cups, several bowls for storing grain. I had made the cups, and they were fine, but they gave me only one *burr* for all. So Auntie and I were waiting, tired from the day, when three Amharas came looking, two men and a woman. They looked at Auntie's huge water jug, which had taken her three days to make. Their mouths showed they praised it.

"You Jews know how to make a vessel," the one man said.

I waited impatiently for the barter to end. With a few coins we would buy embroidery thread and basket-making materials. I had begun my own basket table, a beautiful thing as high as my waist, with straws dyed red, blue, and green to set off the natural color. The table would be mine forever, to bring with me into marriage. I would have worked on it every day, but I always ran out of materials too soon, so I stood with my feet itching, my insides leaping like little frogs, waiting for the trade.

"Well, it looks as if it will hold water well enough." The two men exchanged glances. They wanted that jug. We all knew it was the best to be had anywhere, large and hollow, ringing true, and besides that, beautiful.

"But yet," said the man, still smiling in a way that made

my stomach churn, "the touch of the Jewish *buda* will be locked within the clay forever. And the stink of her Falasha hands."

A bitter taste rose to my throat. I stood there in the sun, the soles of my feet prickling. I wanted to scream out. All my life I heard hateful words like those, but this time I wanted to scream, to break the jar into a thousand pieces, and I stared at my aunt, waiting for her anger to rise as it so often did. But she only bent her head as if she had been beaten, and something in me died forever.

Arrogantly the Amharas flung out the final price. The woman's eyes gleamed with desire. The price was half what the jug would bring at the market in Gondar. We all knew this, just as we all knew it was impossible for my aunt to make her way down to the city where the prices were higher.

Dutifully my aunt handed them the jar and picked up the coins the man left there in the dust.

As they walked away and as the woman strapped the new jug to her back and then continued, arched and swaying, I was filled with hate, and I too knew the lust that brings us to war.

"Ah, well," sighed my aunt. Her head was still bent, her mouth trembling.

My heart sobbed out the words, "Villains! Scoundrels and cheats!" But what can words do, especially when they are only allowed to throb, silently, inside the breast?

Later I could see: This was the moment of my decision. Only I did not realize it yet.

My aunt straightened her back. "Let's go now to buy the straw for your table," she said.

"I don't need it, Auntie," I said through clenched teeth.

Those few coins from the jug might last only for a bit of spice and perhaps the beans we needed for our *wett*.

"You shall have your straw!" she said, her face so fierce that she might have been shouting, but her voice was low.

We went to the man who sold baskets and reeds; he and his wife had watched our humiliation. The wife hid her smile behind her *shamma*. The merchant and his wife were rich indeed with a donkey to carry the loads and a horse to pull a cart. The wife wore a fine embroidered headcloth. They squatted under a canopy raised on two poles against the sun.

As we approached, Aunt Kibret raised her head even higher and she told the man, "Make sure the straw is dry, and the brightest in color, and strong! My niece is making a beautiful table, and only the best will do for her skill." Then piece by piece my aunt picked through the straws, as if she were choosing pieces of gold for a bride gift. I loved her so I thought my heart would burst.

"Well, we don't care about them, and their crazy talk about the Jewish *buda!*" said my aunt, laughing. "If we could really bring the *buda*, wouldn't we use it against our enemies?"

My aunt made fun of them, as is her way, waddling with her walk and shaking her finger. We knew how to laugh, forgetting troubles.

On the way home we sang, happy to be walking light and without the water jars on our backs—um-la-lum-la-lal, ah-la-la! Before we came to our village we bathed in the stream to make ourselves clean, as the Torah commands.

It was good to be together, we two. Auntie had bought real soap at the market. We used it now, making it foam.

"Ah, it is good," she said. "I always wonder why the

other tribes do not like to bathe. They laugh at us and call us the people who smell like water."

"I like smelling like water," I said.

Now I had still heard nothing from Gennet, so when three travelers appeared on the road one day in late fall, I thought there could be news from Gennet, so out I ran from the lean-to, where I was sitting with Almaz picking over raw cotton to remove the seeds.

The men were Beta Yisrael, from the village of M——, and I could see right away they had no good news with them. Their eyes were deep in their faces; they reminded me of the gaunt ghosts that are said to inhabit the mountain caves.

"Almaz! Run for the *kess*," I ordered, and Almaz did so.

Kess Dawit came rushing out of his *tukel* to greet the guests and walk with them across the clearing as courtesy demands, leading them to his home.

By then a small group had gathered, hearing the moans and the lamentations, seeing how the men lifted their hands to heaven, swaying with grief.

"What? What has happened?" The *kess* and the elders wrung their hands, their faces knotted with worry.

The men shook their heads. They trembled. Their eyes showed white; they had seen horrors.

As last they told it in short gasps, words flung out like small explosions. Soldiers. Ripped through the village. Burned the *tukels*. Smashed the roof of the synagogue. Stones now lay in a mound. Piles of stones. Killed. Killed. *They killed the boy! They took our sons.*

I found Joas's face in the crowd of listeners. His nostrils

flared; he stared at me, and his mouth formed the words, "Now. I told you."

"Why? Who were they? What did they want from you?" Kess Dawit spread his arms as if to enfold his brothers. Still they groaned and trembled, their bodies bent with pain, their eyes tracing the memories of what they had seen but could not yet describe.

At last they told it.

"Wild and angry, soldiers came. From the People's Unified Liberation party. They came first for water. They looked exhausted. Hungry, too. We were afraid. We offered them food. Maybe that was our mistake."

"They ate your food?"

"They ate our food. Took our water. It was not enough for them."

The men took deep, painful breaths, reliving it.

"Well, they had been defeated in battle against the Dergue soldiers you see, and had lost numbers of their men. So they were looking not only for food but . . ."

"But for boys," put in his friend. "They wanted our boys for their army."

"Hide your children!" cried the first speaker. "Hide them!"

I gazed at my brother, imagined him looking like these men, bloody and terrified, or worse, captured. Taken by those cruel soldiers, forced to fight, beaten, starved, abused, and finally flung out to the front lines, only to die without even a cause.

I began to move through the crowd. Closer. Closer. To Joas.

"Why did they loot your village?" Gola asked now, gently.

55

"We don't know for sure," one visitor said, but his bright eyes showed the lie. Another held his *shamma* over his temple, and the piece of white cloth was soaked with blood.

"They did it," said the other, "because one of our boys took up a rifle and shot one of the intruder rebels in the chest."

"That boy was his son," explained his kinsman. "The boy escaped then, and the rebels were like wild men—burned the village, shot another boy, took six of our boys to their army, by force."

"And they took two of our women. We heard their screams."

Silence, while we all felt it.

One villager turned to the grieving father and said, "It was not your fault. Your son tried to defend you."

"My son brought their wrath down on all of us. He caused the death of another. I am cursed." He beat his fist against the side of his head.

"You have homes here with us," said Kess Dawit. "Tell your people. You can stay with us as long as you like. We have food, plenty. You are *zamed*, our kin. Come, come, refresh yourselves, bathe your feet. . . ."

So it is among the Beta Yisrael; a brother is always welcome, and every Beta Yisrael is a brother.

I stood beside Joas now, feeling the warmth of his body. His arm touched mine. "After the Segid," he whispered. "What do you say?"

My heart leaped in my chest. "I'm coming with you."

"After the Segid," Joas nodded. "Say nothing yet. I have a plan."

It was only four days more until Segid, the great festival, with other neighboring tribes coming to celebrate with us and stay in our *tukels*.

You see, the world outside can be in confusion, but we Beta Yisrael hold our holy days just the same, so there is order in life. For the first time I thought about Segid, what it really means. It is the celebration of Jews returning from Babylon to Jerusalem, being free.

And I thought, yes, God is calling us, even me, Desta. With signs, he calls me. But maybe it was the *zar* in me, a small devil, that laughed just a little at the same time and said, "Good-bye to Dan, then, farewell to marriage!"

5

ALREADY ON THE MORNING BEFORE THE DAY OF SEGID, IT started. Dawn, and I raised my head to the most terrible shrill screeching that ever was heard in these hills, and ringing all around. Mixed with squawking and plenty of clucks were the shouts of my aunt and a few small boys who had also taken up chasing the chicken.

Oh, how the place shook. I hurried out, pulling my *shamma* close against the early cold, looking out only with my eyes, but was soon unable to stand up straight, bent over from laughter. For the chicken, an old thing whose eggs got smaller and smaller every week until they disappeared entirely—that chicken probably knew from the first moment that this very day would be its last. From the moment my aunt came out to the yard, sharp knife in hand but half-hidden under her dress, I say it—that chicken knew.

Up and squawking, running side to side like a fat old woman, that skinny old chicken swayed, then jumped high as my aunt came upon it with a motion. Whack! But it escaped to the *tukel* of our neighbor who, with the door open, was sleeping still.

Well, my poor aunt bowed down in apology, her face puffed with shame, and standing there to give the proper greetings, "Did you sleep well, neighbor? And are you feeling right this morning? How was your dream? And is your wife well, too, and the children?" Bending and bowing, my aunt was so proper, while the whole time this chicken found a basket hanging on the wall of the neighbor's *tukel* and clung to it, squawking high and shrill to bring down the roof!

Well, at last my aunt got the chicken down and took it, swinging by the neck, to the flat stone where with a sharp force—whack!—she split its neck and, of course with the proper prayer and bleeding-out, gave final grace to this fowl.

Ah, how we laughed, out early in the morning and waiting for the next day when a bit of fat would swim in the pot, for every chicken no matter how skinny still has something good to give.

All that day, of course, we worked at cleaning. We swept the *tukel* until the hard mud floor held not a speck of straw nor a single seed. Out came the skins and the blankets for a vigorous shaking, Almaz on one end and I on the other, pulling them back and forth, jerking and playing, and one time Almaz clung on while I swung her around and around, lifting her even off the ground, and she squealed.

"Enough of this foolishness!" my aunt came out scolding, but laughing, too. There is a right time for foolishness and fun.

We brought out the straw tables and stools and beat them hard, to get out every speck of dust. From the fields we brought leaves to decorate the *tukel,* and lastly we got fresh colors, dipped our hands into the white and the red, and pressed them, so, against the mud-plastered walls, to make handprints that keep out evil. We took our clothes to the stream and washed them white, and we bathed ourselves all over, even our hair, which at last we rubbed with safflower oil to make ourselves gleam so. I looked at Almaz and saw how pretty she was with her little brass earrings and the button she always wears on the thong around her throat. It was given to her at birth, bright blue and with red dots, to protect her from evil.

"Almaz, I love you!" I suddenly said, and caught her, kissing first one cheek and then the other.

She laughed and ran from me, returning then for more kisses again.

Joas and I had not told Almaz about leaving for Jerusalem. Joas was making plans, he said. I looked at Almaz. She was still thin, as always. Nothing we feed her seems to stay on her bones. It is, I think, because as a baby she never got enough mother's milk.

We made special holiday bread of wheat and corn flour mixed together, pouring the dough in spirals over the pan, which lay on hot coals.

Aunt Kibret prepared *wett,* too, with the chicken and a few beans and roots in water, ready to wait the whole next day, for of course we do not cook on Segid, neither do we eat until the holiday is over at sundown. And I thought with a strange emptiness in my chest, when we are gone there will be more food for Uncle and Aunt; they will be glad to have us gone and no longer their responsibility.

But the lie blazed before my eyes like a red-hot coal.

60

The day before Segid, Joas and my uncle stopped working early to go to the stream and bathe with the men, to oil their faces and rub their teeth clean.

All day people came from far away to be with us for Segid, for near our village is a high mountain, with great trees and boulders on the top. There we make a platform for the holy books. We spread woven tapestries between the branches, bright and beautiful, to bring both shade and color.

Early, early the next morning we got up to dress, excited.

"Desta, come here," my aunt called me, sharp.

I had put on my dress, white and clean, and my bracelets, left from my mother. Three of them jingled together on my arm, wide golden hoops, and beautiful.

"Wait," I called back not too loud. A soft voice is always pleasing, but on a holy day, it is commanded. "I am fixing my hair." I had a light blue headcloth to wrap around my hair, and I prepared it in many folds with a knot at the neck, very pretty.

"Come now," said my aunt, softly also, and with a little catching of her breath so that I wondered, What is wrong?

I pushed away the blanket partition and went to where my aunt and uncle slept. Aunt Kibret was kneeling there, taking something white and new from a battered wooden chest she has had forever.

"Put on this *shamma* for the holiday," she said holding it out and watching me, close.

I looked at the cloth, so white and soft, soft as fleece. At the bottom edge of the beautiful new *shamma* was embroidered a thick band of red and white patterns stitched with great care and skill.

"For me?" I breathed.

"Of course for you," my aunt retorted, with her mouth tight, as if she were cross. "Who else is a young girl here, and needing something new and pretty?"

"But when did you make this?" I asked. My breath came in puffs, and my face was all hot with pleasure and surprise. "I never saw you, I never knew."

"Well, there are plenty of days when you are gone in the Margam Bet, aren't you, or going off on some errand? I have had a year to think of it."

A whole year my aunt had been working on this beautiful *shamma*, and just for me! I kissed her again and again, cheek to cheek, and she laughed until she pushed me lightly away, saying "Go on now, and let me finish dressing, and get Almaz ready, too, so we can leave with the others, all together."

Of course we would leave with the others! How else would we go up the mountain to the Segid, if not with all our *zamed* and friends and neighbors and kinsmen from other villages? The boys were so serious and proud, some of them allowed to carry the Torah. The *kessim*, wearing their holiday *shammas*, brought thick walking sticks, for the mountain was rough with rocks and ruts. Kess Dawit, tall and mighty holding his staff, looked like a shepherd. And then of course, there were our guards, watching.

The women walked together, all in finery, wearing their best beads and gold chains and bracelets, to make the air jingle so. My aunt wore her betrothal earrings and pendant, gold over brass, and I had never seen her more beautiful. Her holiday dress was embroidered at the neck, and with it her holiday *shamma* had the same matching stitches, wide and in three rows of design. She wore sandals of leather,

62

saved for special days like these, and carried her bright pink parasol high over her head.

A certain fragrance drifted out over the hills; I remember it still. As we neared the top of the mountain, all talk ceased. A breeze blew softly. Slim weeds bent under its touch, and tiny seeds blew about. Leaves rustled under our feet, and this sound together with the jingling of the women's jewels and the soft sighing breath of those who labored on the climb— all this brought music to the heart.

Turning, I saw below me and also above a long line of my people, all in their white *shammas*, walking up. The little boys were dressed variously, in short pants and shirts under their *shammas*, some with belts and brass buckles, all put together differently, with colors and patches and pieces of cloth torn away, but they looked beautiful in their seriousness, their devotion. Some of the old people carried large stones on their shoulders. The stones were heavy, like their sins, to be discarded and forgotten once they reached the mountain-top. Glorious day! The day to celebrate the giving of the Torah! The Torah is our law and our life.

As we reached the top of the hill, the people spread out, men first, close to the *kessim*. We women stayed back, then touched our foreheads to the ground in prayer.

We stood quietly through the long, long reading, even the babies wrapped in the slings on their mothers' backs, all covered with the white *shammas*, their little brown faces peeking out, listening hard or sometimes fast asleep. Now and then a mother brought a squirming little one around and to her breast; it suckled, then slept, while everyone continued to listen, standing under the shade of a parasol or a tree, the priests' words blending with the rustling leaves: "This is thy God that brought thee up out of Egypt. . . . yea, forty years did God sustain us in the wilderness, and we lacked nothing. . . . He came down also upon Mount Sinai and spoke with the people from heaven and gave them right ordinances and laws of truth. . . ."

And I prayed hard, my eyes shut tight, "Lord, protect Joas and Almaz and me on the trek. Though we walk through the wilderness, be with us, as You were with Moses."

Kess Dawit read the Ten Commandments, and he read again from the Bible how the Jews were released from captivity in Babylon and how they returned to Jerusalem to rebuild the Temple.

Joas said he had a plan; what was it? Did he have a guide for us? I knew we could not find our way out alone; but my brother is smart. He had gone to the village of Kess Haim and Dan, probably for advice. Probably the *kess* had helped him find a guide, someone who could be trusted.

I looked at Joas, saw him listening to the prayers. We all chanted the responses.

Then came the sermon, and the *kess* from the village of M—— delivered it, saying that we must remain faithful to Torah; the reward of the keeping the law he said, is Jerusalem. "Be steadfast in your faith!" he cried, staff uplifted. "Keep yourselves pure, for your return to Zion." The same words from year to year, but this time with new meaning.

I caught a glimpse of Dan, stern as usual. He stood by his father, deep in prayer, with no eyes for anyone else. I wondered, Would I have to return the betrothal pendant to Dan? I knew of nobody who had ever broken a betrothal, but had heard about such a thing only when it was shown that the girl was no longer a virgin, and the young man demanded his gifts back. Well, maybe I would keep the pendant. Why think about it? It is Segid, after all, time for joy!

Afternoon, we rested under the trees, women together, all talking softly and laughing, and babies there, plenty. How I love babies! Meanwhile, the men prayed and prayed, never stopping, bending and swaying in prayer, and their voices rang out over us so that we felt everything was safe.

But of course it was not so. Even while we prayed, six of our men stood aside with rifles to guard the people.

Late afternoon, we saw three men, spies. They were from the Peasants' Association, and one official from town wearing a necktie. How strange! The tie hung short over the man's round belly, very wide, yellow with red dots. Ah, how he boasted of that tie, pushing it out on his belly.

They stood watching with their bright eyes, and then we saw four others at the edge of our crowd, like warriors and evil; Something different came into our service now, a stiff feeling, danger.

At last the sun sank down, and the small horn was blown to announce the return of the priests and the Torah from the mountain.

The priests went down first, holding the Torahs high, and we followed all in procession, joyful in spite of the grim officials. How could we let them spoil our day?

Down the mountain everyone came single file, and those already in the village began to sing, leaping high into the air. They were Ethiopian songs of revolution, to please the grim men from the association; you can hold your Jewish festival, was the understanding. But afterward you must also give us our due. So they stood listening while we sang out:

Ethiopia, Ethiopia, arise.
Hail to the party and the motherland,
Hail and hope for tomorrow!

The man with the wide tie waved for everyone to come to a circle, to sit down, for now he would speak and he needed listeners. Well, we sat down on the ground, and he talked about Ethiopia, how lucky we were for this beautiful land, how we must always be faithful and never, never leave. "Look how good things are for you!" he shouted, hands in the air. "You have food for your children, fresh water, and nobody bothers you. Land has been given to everyone; our government is not only for the rich, but for all. Hail to the Glorious Revolution!" he cried, his hands high.

We echoed politely. "Hail to the revolution!"

"We are Ethiopians, all together, all the same," he shouted. "Some people would have you think you might find happiness somewhere else. Among white people. Never! Never! Black, we are brothers. Only we can understand each other; the white devils have never meant us any good. One Ethiopia! One brotherhood!" he shouted, his arms raised high.

When he was finished we all clapped politely, and still it was tense, with some babies howling so.

At last the association men were satisfied. They had brought a broken-down small van, the engine stinking and coughing loud, but proudly they crowded into it, heads high and nodding their wealth to us while we waited for them to disappear.

After that we all began to sing, not songs of revolution, but our own. We laughed at the man with his wide tie; some of the boys made signs with their hands imitating him, and everyone rolling with laughter, happy now for the feast that would soon start. On Segid and other special days we all eat together. Every family brings what it can, a little or a lot, and nobody knows who brought what.

After we had eaten someone began to sing. A drumbeat came, then more music, from cymbals, gongs, and the one stringed violin. The singing grew louder, fuller, more joyful, and several got up to dance, shoulders moving vigorously, and hips, too.

Stars were spread above us, so many, and in the far edges of the hills we heard the soft howling of beasts while we were safe here and warm by the fire. I looked around, and I knew every face and every name, the little children with whom I have played, Almaz's friends and my friends, both girls and boys, that I have known since we were babies. I saw the women with whom I have bathed and joked and shared gossip every day of my life, and so much laughter. I sang and swayed my head to the beat of the drum, and I thought how I love them!

Joas calling, took my arm and brought me up to dance in the line, woman to woman, facing the men opposite, and all dancing, swaying, shoulders and hips and heads matching beat for beat. The beat struck, faster, the movements free, as if we have known them forever, and we danced, danced, until we were panting and ready to drop, all of us young people together.

As we sat together, family, very close, Dan came with

his father and brothers and Weizero Channa, so old with her face shrunken and hair whispy white. Weizero Channa touched my head as I kissed her knee in respect.

Now came all the inquiries about everybody's health, smiling and bowing, and Dan looked at me and said, "Hello, Desta, and happy holidays to you."

"Thank you, Dan, and to you," I said, looking down. I felt everyone's eyes upon me, burning my face, but still I was proud, looking fine in my new *shamma* and with bracelets.

"Soon there will be a wedding, eh?" said Weizero Channa, smiling and nodding. "A new family in a new land."

I glanced up, startled.

"We are going to Jerusalem," said Dan's father gravely.

Now the two families crowded close, close together. Kess Haim laid his hand on Uncle Tekle's arm; Weizero Channa's face was close to Aunt Kibret's.

"You are going?" Uncle Tekle nodded. "When?"

"We are getting everything ready," said Kess Haim. "Food. Water. We have some money for a guide. And we are making a litter for Weizero Channa."

"But," said Uncle Tekle, "how can you think of carrying Weizero Channa so far? Down the mountain is . . . is . . . hard," he stammered, "the cliffs are steep and then the desert . . ."

"Weizero Channa is old," said the *kess*. "She wants to lay her head down finally in Jerusalem." Now he clasped Uncle Tekle's shoulder. "She is my mother," he said. "How can I deny her this wish? After I have brought her to Jerusalem, I will return, then help to lead out others. Soon," he said, "there will be no Jews left in Ethiopia. Come with us, Tekle!"

My uncle shook his head. "Haim, you know I could never walk so far."

"But with a mule, Tekle . . ."

"Who is so rich as to own a mule, Haim? You honor me too greatly."

"Well, a crutch. Maybe with a crutch."

"I am needed here," Uncle Tekle said. "Haim, I cannot travel. Besides, some of us must stay here."

Kess Haim nodded. "My oldest son, Yona, is remaining to take my place as *kess* in our village. But, Tekle, think of it! We have come at last to the days of the prophets. Everything that was foretold is happening now. It's happening now!"

"And Dan is going with you to Jerusalem?"

"Dan is coming with me to take his grandmother to Jerusalem. Then Dan will stay in the holy city. He will make his life there. I know your children, too, are going. Joas has spoken to us about it. The young men have made the plan these many months. I know how proud you must be of your nephew."

My uncle pulled the edge of his *shamma* over his mouth to conceal what he felt.

Kess Haim continued, "Who would have thought that we would be the ones, in our lifetime, to be so blessed?"

"Quite true," said my uncle faintly, and my aunt's fingers gripped me once, tight, then released me.

"When they reach Israel," said Dan's father, "Dan and Desta must be married at once. I will make the marriage myself. Don't you agree?"

"Of course," said my uncle.

Kess Haim put his hand on my shoulder. I felt the weight

of it. "So God has ordained," the *kess* said, as if he could look into my wicked mind, "that Desta and Dan will begin their new lives together in Israel."

I had no breath to reply. I bent my head, felt Kess Haim's hand upon it in blessing.

From the branches of a tall gum tree I heard the sudden croak of a parrot, like the wild laughter of a little *zar*.

6

THAT NIGHT THE LAMP BURNED LATE IN OUR *TUKEL*.

"You went behind our backs to talk to Kess Haim? To Dan? To make plans to leave?" My aunt was shocked.

"I talked to the *kess*," said Joas, "just as I have talked to you about it every day, but you do not hear. We must leave. Kess Haim says it, too. And after the raid on the village of M——"

"It is true, Kibret," said Uncle Tekle. "We cannot hold them or hide them here forever. You know it."

"And who will look after Desta on the trip? A young girl . . ."

"I will look after her," said Joas. "And we'll be safe traveling with the *kess* and others."

Aunt Kibret sat down on the ledge, her body sagging. She had been standing before us, furious, with hands on her hips. Now she sat down softly, pulling at the fringe of her sash.

"I am of two minds," she said at last. "I am afraid for

them. But also I want them to go. Their mother and father would have wanted it." She moistened her lips, waiting. "For weeks now, in the night, I hear their voices telling me, 'let them go!' "

"And so we must," said Uncle Tekle, "with our blessing."

"What about Almaz?" I was the one who said it, though we were all thinking it.

"She is so small yet," said Aunt Kibret instantly.

"She is not strong," said Uncle Tekle.

"In Israel," said Joas firmly, "Almaz will get strong. And on the way, I will carry her when she gets tired."

Well, it went on, but we all knew how it would end. My mother died giving Almaz to us for a sister; Almaz was of our blood, ours to take, to save, to bring to Jerusalem. Nobody, not even our aunt and uncle, our dearest and closest *zamed* had the right to keep her from us. It is good we did not need to tell them this; they knew.

"Almaz is your sister," Aunt Kibret said, "and she belongs with you if you will care for her."

"I will protect her with my life," said Joas.

"And I, too," I promised.

Aunt Kibret went to the jar where coins are kept. She reached inside, folded some coins into a cloth, made a knot, and gave it to me, pressing it into my hand.

I felt the weight of the coins, and I started to protest.

"Well, I will tell you," said my aunt, "I think your uncle and I will move to town when you are gone. We have wanted this for a long time, but with children, well, it is not so easy."

72

Joas and I looked at each other. Uncle Tekle's brows were raised in that look of shock and surprise. Oh, how my aunt will talk!

"What would Uncle do there?" I asked.

Joas gave me a nudge. They would never move to town; it was just her way, to pretend to have plans of her own.

"Oh, he is a blacksmith, isn't he? He can fix tools, maybe learn to mend buses. Even cars. Cars break, and they need to be fixed."

So plans were made. In three days we would leave for the village where Dan lived—Joas, Almaz, and I. Also going were four other young people from our village and two grown-ups. The six others were setting off a day early, to go to market at T——, getting supplies for the trip. We would all meet at Dan's village and travel together with the guide hired by Kess Haim.

"So by next month," my aunt said, smiling wide, "you will already be in Jerusalem!"

"But . . . but you . . ." I stammered, tearful.

"We will be safe in the city!" my aunt exclaimed. "And getting rich from Uncle's work, so soon we can fly to you in Jerusalem, don't you see? Maybe the government will change and let us go. Why not? Times are changing. Yes, I feel it."

My dear, brave aunt!

Three days together, to get ready and to live the time minute by minute, trying not to think: *This is the last time washing in this stream, the last time bringing up water, the last time grinding* teff *on this mortar, the last time, last time . . .*

I helped Almaz wash her clothes, even the extra dress,

and as we scrubbed she talked and talked.

"Will Aunt and Uncle really come to us later?"

"Yes, yes," I said, "why not?"

"Because Uncle can hardly walk," she said.

"Well, they will fly to us in a plane, then," I said.

"I never heard of anybody who did that."

"Petros did. And the white visitors. They had to, to get here. Almaz, don't you know anything?" I shook my head, impatient. Then I looked at her, bent over her washing, so small and so thin. "Almaz," I said, "the main reason we are going to Jerusalem is so that we can learn. When we get there, you will go to school. So will I."

"But you are getting married," she said. "How can you go to school?" she asked, turning wide-eyed to see my reply.

How indeed?

"Desta! I want to talk to you."

Aunt Kibret's voice startled us. She had come to the stream with her water jug and stood watching us, as we now realized.

"Almaz," she said, with a motion of her head, "go and prepare some tea for our supper." She set the jug down for Almaz.

"It's so early yet, Auntie," Almaz objected.

"Go!" said my aunt. "Obey me."

Aunt Kibret helped me lay out our garments in the sun. Then she said, "Let's walk."

We walked, leaving the stream behind us, beyond the women's hut, over to a small hill, from which we could see down into the valley and beyond it, ridge upon ridge of mountains ever descending, with spirals and platforms cut into the slopes, each layer of a different color. We sat down on a rock, both of us in the same posture, elbows bent, hands to our cheeks, and slightly swaying.

"It is beautiful here, isn't it?" said Aunt Kibret after a time.

"Yes."

"Do not forget these moments," she said, "when you are gone in Jerusalem. It has not all been so bad."

"Surely not!" I cried, thinking of all the times with Aunt Kibret, laughing, working, eating, talking. "Does Jerusalem look like this, do you think?"

Aunt Kibret shook her head, smiling. "Desta, I don't know about such things. I am a plain woman, never gone to school, not for a single day. I only know that these mountains are beautiful, and that when the hawk flies, so . . ." and she lifted her arm, pointing to the beautiful bird as it bent to the wind, ". . . I feel my heart flying up to the sky. Do you see?"

"Yes, I see." She meant more than just the hawk, I knew.

"Dan wanted to marry you before the journey," Aunt Kibret said.

"He did?"

"His father would not allow it."

"Why?"

Aunt Kibret smiled. "Why did he want to marry you, or why did his father forbid it?"

"Both," I said, shaking my head, but smiling, too. I knew the *kess* had planned on our marrying in Jerusalem but I did not know there had been much talk about it.

75

"Well, to marry you now would hardly leave sufficient time to consummate your marriage."

I felt embarrassed.

"It is written," my aunt continued, "that the young bridegroom must spend time with his wife and make her happy. Take her to him. Do you understand?"

I nodded. "Yes." I felt a flash of relief. I wanted to be with my brother, with the other young people, and free. I looked down, hiding my eyes and the relief that must have shown in them.

"Also, Dan is needed now to bring his grandmother to Jerusalem. It is a holy task. Kess Haim said that Dan could not be thus divided and of two minds, one with his grandmother to take to the holy land and also a new wife to worry about."

"So we are still to marry in Israel," I said.

"Yes."

"Who will give me away?"

My aunt took my arm, pulling my hand from my cheek, so that she could look at me. "Your mother and father have given you, long ago," she said. "Your uncle and I have agreed, and we have sealed it again with Dan's father. So you are given, Desta, surely and forever."

Tears stung my eyes. I did not like the idea of being given, like a woven cloth or a piece of *injera*. "Who will be there at my wedding?" I said, challenging her.

"You mean Uncle and me?" she gasped, then said firmly, "Desta, you may wait a short time. Then, however, your brother will take you to Dan's house, wherever he is in Jerusalem. And the two of you will be married by Kess Haim.

Your brother and sister will be there. And your friends from the village. We will come to you when we can. You know that. It could take time. Meanwhile, you must do what is right."

I said nothing, hoping inside that in Jerusalem things might be different as Alemu had said that day in the Margam Bet.

"Do you hear me?" Kibret admonished.

"Yes, I hear. And what about Almaz?"

"Dan will also take Almaz into his home. This has been talked about and agreed upon. Of course, Desta, you will also have to look after Weizero Channa. She is old and frail. You will be her granddaughter, and giving her all due respect and help. Isn't it so?" she said sharply.

"Yes," I said, my eyes downcast, voice low. My life, it seemed, was already tied to a track, the way an ox is tied to a millstone or to a plow.

"I see in your eyes something unworthy," said my aunt. She gave my wrist a sharp tap. "Out with it! It is ugly when you hold anger that way, and rebellion, Desta. I have talked to you about this before."

"I only wonder," I said, making my tone soft, "how I shall go to school and learn Hebrew—and you said I was to learn—if I am taking care of everybody, cooking and cleaning and tending babies in the house."

My aunt sighed, and she shook her head. "You will learn as your husband teaches you, Desta. You will learn enough that you can go to market and buy what you need. Maybe other women will teach you their skills. Weaving. Cooking. All the things you need to know."

77

"I had thought to learn other things," I protested.

"What other things can be of use to you?" Aunt Kibret exclaimed. "Ah, how to care for babies, yes, how to tend a sick husband . . . all this you will learn. If you apply yourself. Desta, be a woman, truly."

We sat looking down over the hills. A partridge fluttered in circles near our feet, making small clucking sounds.

"Well," my aunt said at last, "times change. It is true that women are going to school, learning letters, the way you started to do in the village school. Is that what you want, Desta? To read?"

"Oh, yes, Auntie!" I leaped to my feet, catching her arms. I had not realized I wanted it so much. "In Addis Ababa there are newspapers, plenty, and other things to read. Joas has told me. It will be that way in Jerusalem, too, I know it. I want to be able to read them, to know things, to be able to speak to all the people in their languages. Can't I?"

Aunt Kibret smiled. "Well, well, I suppose there might even be schools for married women, where they can read, and books for them, too."

She stood up beside me now, and leaning toward me, my aunt kissed me first on one cheek, then on the other. "You are a good girl, Desta," she said. "And tomorrow night, I will tell about you, how you are in my heart."

We were to eat together with all the villagers on that very last night. They would say prayers for our safe journey, and our family and friends would tell things about us, our habits, our ways, to keep us each firm in the minds of our *zamed*, and there would be kissing, plenty.

* * *

If it had been as planned, if we had had that last farewell, if we had been able to leave with dignity . . . a plan is one thing, reality another. It did not happen the way we thought, and when we left it was in haste and with shouting, no time to think and no looking back.

Midmorning of that last day, everything was as usual. Almaz and I were preparing *injera* for the journey, water stood ready in the jugs, and everything cleanly packed—still we had the night to think about, and the feasting with our *zamed*.

Suddenly from the hilltop came a shout, and our village boys came running. "Soldiers! Soldiers! We have seen them among the trees, making their way up the road."

"Who are they?" Uncle Tekle shouted, holding his hammer aloft.

"Not Dergue," said one boy. "Maybe the Liberation Front."

"What's the difference?" shouted Joas, distracted and grasping a rifle. "We all know what they will do."

"You must leave now," said Uncle Tekle. His eyes were wild. He gave Joas a slight push. "Joas! Take your sisters and go."

Aunt Kibret pulled me inside the lean-to beside our *tukel*. "Desta, we have no time now to say good-bye," she said, her tone swift and eyes hard. "Take this water jug and your things. Do you have the money?"

"Auntie, we are not going until tomorrow!"

"Foolish girl!" she cried, giving me a shake. "Have you lost your senses? The soldiers are coming. Do you think they will let you simply walk out of here tomorrow? Go! Everything is ready. Go!"

Then Joas was beside me with Almaz clinging to him

and a bulky bundle tied to his back, a rifle sticking out.

"Joas," I breathed. "Can't we hide?"

"God keep you, Desta," said my uncle, kissing me quickly, giving me a slight push. "Joas. My boy." Uncle Tekle embraced him. "Keep to the high road! Take care of them, Joas!"

"Yes, yes, Uncle."

"Go quickly," he said, his eyes upon us.

"What about the others?" I cried.

"They'll find their way," my aunt shot back. "They will meet you at Dan's village. Go."

"Aunt Kibret! I want to take my table." I made a lunge toward the *tukel*. She held me back.

"No."

"I want it!" The table was nearly finished now, and truly mine.

"Desta, please, you can't carry all that. You must take this skin," said my aunt, thrusting it upon me.

"Auntie, I don't need it!"

"For Almaz!" she hissed. "She is always cold. Go now, for God's sake!" Looking into my face my aunt shouted, "I will bring you the table when I come to you. I promise. Now, go!"

Pushed by their words, by the urgency in their faces, and by their hands, we ran.

7

"WE'RE GOING THE WRONG WAY," I PANTED, WHEN AT LAST we were far enough from the village to allow ourselves to speak. I tried not to think of the soldiers, what they might do.

"This is a diversion," said Joas. "We cannot take the direct road." With his long legs he has an easy ambling gait, even uphill.

"It will take longer," I said.

"Desta, I used to take this road to go to school. I know it better than you. It is not longer, but shorter." It was true, Joas had made the trip often, staying in the village all week to study, returning home for Shabbat. How I used to envy him that schooling!

"A harder climb," I muttered. "It will take longer with me and Almaz—you climb like an ibex. We are only human."

"Then save your breath for the climb," Joas ordered. "I know a cave where we can rest. There we'll wait. It's better to travel in the dark."

"I don't want to travel in the dark!" Almaz cried.

Joas silenced her with a fierce look. Then he turned to me and said firmly, "I am the leader here."

Almaz was frightened; she kept asking questions under her breath, her voice catching in a kind of sob. "Where are we going? Where will we sleep tonight? I don't want to sleep near any hyenas."

"Be quiet, Almaz," Joas said. "Look, I will tell you something. Remember how I told you I used to go to school?"

"Yes."

"Well, that school was brought up the mountain piece by piece on the backs of donkeys. What do you think of that?"

"I don't believe you," said Almaz, sullen.

"When we get to the village I will show it to you," said Joas.

We climbed nearly straight up, bending low as we walked, keeping ourselves under the cover of bushes. It was not the sort of road soldiers would take. Still, we had to be careful. Joas is smart, I admitted to myself, though wishing he were not so commanding.

What was happening at home? Had the soldiers come through the village, and had they gone on a rampage? We asked each other only with our eyes; we had all the questions, none of the answers. The soldiers could take anything they wanted—food, young boys for the army, or girls for their pleasure. Anything could happen—or nothing. Sometimes the soldiers passed us by, or they might only ask for water. Sometimes they have even been kind, bringing us information about a new clinic.

I looked at Joas in his old military coat. He had told me that in Israel he would join the army. He said it is a fine army, and I would be proud. For me, I would be happy never to see a rifle again.

Joas went ahead of us, turning every little while to stand still with his hand shading his eyes, looking all around. He would hold up his hand, warning us to silence, and I whispered to Almaz, "If anyone comes, get into the brush and lie perfectly still, do you hear?"

"There are brambles in the bushes," she objected.

"Quiet! Don't be such a baby."

I looked at Joas standing there, so tall and so sure. He scanned the hills and the boulders; I saw his nostrils flare as he breathed of the air, seeking traces of something human.

He motioned us onward. We grew hot from climbing, and when we passed a small pool nestled between tall green reeds, I rushed over, ready to dip my feet in the cool water. Joas grabbed my shoulder, hard.

"No," he said sternly.

"I want to bathe!"

"The water is not clean," he said. "Look, how sluggish it lies, can't you see? If you bathe here, you will be sick."

I shrugged off his hand. I knew he was right; in some waters there are parasites that can squirm in under the skin to make people itch until they think they would rather die.

"Desta, you have to be careful what you do," Joas said heavily. "I cannot watch you every minute. And you are responsible for Almaz. I don't want you to drink anything, do you hear, unless you ask me first. Do you hear?"

"Yes," I said, my tone meek, but my heart hammering

with anger. I do not like to be wrong; I hate it when he talks to me that way. It would not be an easy journey with my brother; I was glad we were meeting the others soon.

At last we got to the cave, and now instead of steaming in the heat, we sat and shivered.

"Can't we continue to Dan's village now?" I asked Joas, after we had sat for some time, gaining our breath. "It's cold waiting here."

"No," Joas said. "We'll wait. Sleep a while. We can share a cake of *injera* first." He held out his hand. "Give it to me."

"*Injera?*" I was numb with dread.

"Yes, yes, we have had nothing all day, and I am hungry."

"Joas," I said quietly, "I don't have any food."

"But of course you do!" Angrily Joas tore the bulky pack from my arms, shaking out my extra dress and the new holiday *shamma* Aunt Kibret had given me for Segid. He fingered through the cloth tied around my golden hoop bracelets and the few coins, and then he shook out the skin that Aunt Kibret had pressed upon me in the last moment.

"You are useless," Joas said flatly, sitting down and turning his face away from me, angry.

"It wasn't my fault!" I cried. "The soldiers were coming. We weren't going to leave until tomorrow. Aunt Kibret should have given it to me."

"Almaz," Joas said sternly. "Did you bring food?"

"No! Nobody gave me any food. Don't you have it? You two?"

I said. "Now we have to go on to the village."

Joas glared at me. "It was your job to bring food, to remember it, no matter how quickly we left," he cried. "How dare you blame it on Aunt Kibret? Why weren't you thinking to provide food for us? You are the mother now, the woman among us. It is your task to bring the food!"

I felt a terrible sinking feeling inside. I could not even move or think.

For a long time we sat in silence, our angers circling around us like evil spirits, each of us separate and furious.

"We can each have a sip of water from the jug," Joas said at last. "There is water in it, Desta, isn't there?" he said sharply. "Surely, you did remember that."

All day I had been carrying that huge water jug strapped to my back; of course there was water in it! "What do you think?" I cried angrily. "That my back bends and aches from carrying an empty jug?"

"Don't fight anymore," said Almaz softly, making a tiny chirping sound like a bird. "You frighten the animals."

Joas and I both began to laugh. "What animals?" we asked, laughing and then feeling better from it.

We drank a little water, and we laid down with our heads on our bundles, Joas close to the mouth of the cave with his rifle ready.

I must have fallen asleep. A sudden movement startled me, and I sat up straight. It was dark inside the cave.

"What?" I cried.

"We can go home now," came Almaz's voice, ringing from the hollowness of the cave.

"What are you talking about?" I exclaimed, reaching out in the darkness to catch her. I took hold of her dress, pulled her over. "We're not going back. Didn't you know that?"

Almaz started to wail like a funeral, and Joas rushed to us, harshly scolding, "Quiet! Be quiet!"

"I don't want to leave them!" Almaz wailed, doubled over and beating her hands into the air. "You never asked me, you just pulled me away. I don't want to go anywhere!"

"Can't you keep her quiet?" Joas cried.

"Maybe the soldiers are gone now," Almaz wailed. "We can go back! I want to go back!"

I struck out and slapped Almaz on the cheek; the blow fell half on her temple, and she cringed, howling all the harder.

"Quiet," I said then harshly, and I shook her until her sobs grew lighter.

"Behave yourself," I commanded, giving her a final shake, then letting her go.

"Don't tell me what to do," Almaz said suddenly in a voice filled with hate, as if a *zar* had entered her body.

I hit her again, deliberately. "You must do everything I say from now on. Do you hear me?"

Joas stood beside us, and he pulled Almaz to her feet. "It is true," he said, his voice firm.

Almaz slept at last. Joas came to me in the darkness, whispering. "We must keep her quiet," he said. "We must make her keep moving."

"I know," I whispered back. "Were we right to bring her with us? We could leave her in Dan's village, you know. They would take care of her, or bring her back to Auntie."

"Is that what you want to do?" he asked.

"No."

"Neither do I."

I covered Almaz and me with the skin, tight, and slept until Joas shook me, too soon.

"We'll go now," he said firmly.

"I'm too tired," I replied, stretching, then pulling myself back into a ball, warm against Almaz's small body.

"We have to change our habits," Joas said, "and learn to sleep in the day. Do you understand?" He shook me harder.

I stood up, pulled my clothes into proper order, and got Almaz awake.

"I wish we had a lamp," I whispered as we edged our way out of the cave and met blackness outside. There was only the small trace of a moon, a sliver.

"I wish we had a goat," Joas joked. It is an old family joke, the story of a man who is never satisfied, wishing first for a sip of water, then for some milk, then for a cheese, for meat stew, and finally for the whole goat, until the goat kicks over the water jug and the whole thing starts again.

We walked on in the darkness. Joas has eyes like a cat.

"I wonder what happened in the village," Almaz said once.

"Maybe they only stopped for water by our stream," Joas said. "At least we are on our way."

Near dawn we found some berries, wet with dew from the night. "Don't eat too many or too fast," I warned Almaz.

"I won't," she said, subdued.

But a short time later she slipped behind some bushes, and I heard her groaning, and when she returned to us her face was drawn tight with pain.

We watched the sun come up; It seemed an omen when a beam of light settled suddenly upon a rift in the hills, shining down to bring out the deep emerald colors and to touch the tiny yellow daisies lodged in between the rocks.

We rested then among a cluster of boulders, huddled in our *shammas*, for it was cold, and the earth still damp from the night. My stomach growled.

"I wish I had some nuts," I murmured.

"I wish I had a goat," said Joas.

"I wish you two would stop wishing," said Almaz.

We were content, with Joas to protect us, the rifle laid across his knees. From a tree overhead we heard scurrying sounds.

"Monkeys," said Almaz.

Almaz has a keen ear for such things, and an eye, too. She was right. Moments later we heard them chattering above us, and soon we saw furry streaks flying from one limb to the next.

I glanced at Joas. He looked tired. "Aren't you ever going to sleep?"

"I'm not tired," he said.

"Why did Uncle give you his rifle?" Almaz asked.

"He can get himself another," Joas replied.

"Do you have bullets?" Almaz continued.

"Yes."

"How many?" I asked.

"Plenty," Joas said.

"How many?" I repeated.

"Nine."

Nine bullets. Well.

"Desta," Joas said, "until we get to Jerusalem, I will be the master."

I nodded. Although I hated his commanding, it is true, any group needs order.

"Even when we meet the *kess* and the others, you and Almaz are my *zamed*. You must listen to me and not ask questions."

"I know, Joas."

He sat back, fingering the two buttons on his coat. "In Israel," he said, his eyes half-closed, dreaming, "I will learn fast. I already know some Hebrew. Then I will go into the army. I'll get a new coat and a cap and boots, a fine rifle. Do you know they have machine guns? I'll help to patrol the borders. I'll have friends, plenty, among the soldiers. Desta, even girls are soldiers in Israel. Did you know that?"

I laughed. "No," I said. "I do not believe it."

Joas laughed too, pulling me up. "Well then, you'll just have to see for yourself. The day will come when little Almaz will be a soldier, too. Come on, let's hurry. The sooner we get there the sooner our stomachs will be full again."

As guests of the village, food would be given us generously; I could hardly wait. I wondered when we would start out on the trek, how many of us there would be, and what provisions. They would probably have several mules, as needed to carry old Weizero Channa on her litter. Maybe there would even be an extra mule, and maybe Almaz could ride it sometimes when she got tired walking.

So we went on, walking faster and faster as we approached. The last part of the way was a gradual slope upwards, ever up, until we stood at the top of a rock ridge looking down to Dan's village nestled amid trees and wide fields, very beautiful. I had never approached from this side before;

it was breathtaking, splendid, also exciting to climb down those cliffs, with the knees feeling pinched, our toes clinging to the rocks, and holding on always with one hand.

"Don't look down!" I warned Almaz.

She giggled and looked down on purpose, shrieking with delight. Well, we are used to such climbing; Almaz is nimble as a little monkey herself.

Down, down we hurried, bringing rocks and gravel and dirt down behind us, skidding, sliding, laughing, until we were flat at last, and seeing a stream now we hurried to it, to lay ourselves down flat and taste the sweet rushing water, drinking deep.

We washed our hands and our faces, then set out on the road that leads to the houses.

"There is the school," said Joas, pointing. "You see? I told you."

"Why is it boarded up?" asked Almaz.

"Because the government won't let us have schools anymore, you know that," said Joas crossly. "But it was a fine school," he added with pride. "Look, they even made a well out front, for the pupils to drink clean water."

As we passed the school we saw strange letters engraved on a wooden beam over the entrance: ORT.

"What does that mean, Joas?"

"It is the name of the group that gave us the school," Joas said with a shrug. "That's all I know."

Now a cluster of *tukels* came into view, a few goats grazing and bleating, and some chickens scratching, out early.

But no *kess* came to greet us, no elders, nobody. The village looked strangely asleep. The first person we saw was

90

a woman, coming up with water from the stream, and her three little girls all carrying jugs, too.

We greeted the woman politely, then asked for the *kess*.

She looked at us, squinting, then she shook her head.

"But they are gone," she said. "They left after dark last night and took old Weizero Channa with them."

"How many?" asked Joas, barely moving his lips.

"Kess and Weizero, and others from our village," said the woman, while the little girls stared at us, "and six from the village of S—— came in at sundown to meet them. All left together and took old Weizero Channa on a litter."

Joas seemed unable to move. "They left without us?" he said at last, shaking his head. "They left without us?"

The woman nodded. "The guide said they had to leave now. He would not wait. A stormy fellow, in a hurry, plenty. Who knows why? Kess Haim could not hold him."

"Which way did they go?" asked Joas.

"Are you from the village of S——?"

"Yes, of course!" cried Joas, distracted now beyond courtesy, and I looked down in shame for him, while the little girls still stared, wide-eyed.

"Well, they said they would look for you and find you on the road. They thought with your sisters you would be coming slow and be on the road to meet them sometime."

"They took the main road?" Joas asked, disbelieving.

"Of course. Why didn't you meet them? How did you come here?"

Joas pointed. "The opposite way. Down the cliffs."

The woman shook her head, wide-eyed, as if we must be crazy.

"If we hurry," said Joas, "we can still catch up."

"Won't you have something to eat?" asked the woman, her face furrowed, eyes in a squint.

"No, thank you," said Joas. "We can't stay."

"But you must eat! My neighbors will think me stingy! We have *wett* and *tella,* and *injera,* plenty, plenty. Chickpeas and pepper, you must have some."

Even Almaz stood quietly, shaking her head, and I looked down at my feet, my mouth watering.

"We thank you for your generous hospitality," said Joas. "But I am sorry, we must leave right away and catch up with the others. We promised our uncle we'd go with them. It is his wish. Please forgive us." So saying, Joas pulled me away.

I could hardly believe we were leaving the village, and without food. None! My stomach rumbled out loud in protest.

Brother, I thought, you are the rudest person in creation! But I said nothing. I knew better.

8

WE HAD GONE ONLY A LITTLE WAY, AND I WAS SCOWLING BUT decided to say nothing for once, to leave the fighting inside me. I thought I would never speak to Joas again. Soon we heard a call, a high childish voice, and then we saw the three little girls behind us, hot from running.

"Wait! Wait! We packed you something for your journey."

We stopped, smiling and happy to greet the children who were beaming with pleasure at their own goodness. Each girl carried a bundle on her hip, one a small sack of *teff*, the other some beans with peppers already cooked, and the third a loaf of *musvat*, the special Sabbath bread made from wheat. The smell of it, crusty on the outside, warm and doughy on the inside, made me weak with desire.

We thanked the girls with smiles and bows, and Almaz ran up to the youngest of them and kissed her soundly on both cheeks. Then the other two had to get their kisses, and I watched, smiling, admiring Almaz and her way, like a puppy, winning people to her always.

The girls climbed into a tree and sat watching us as we went, like monkeys clinging there. We turned once more and waved good-bye before we were out of their valley, going down around the other side to the main road.

I had not traveled here before, but the hooves of innumerable donkeys and mules, together with the footprints of men bent on trading between villages had carved out a narrow trail. We would follow it to the main road, there surely to meet the others.

"We will eat later," said Joas.

Of course, I thought, still silent, though feeling much better with the fresh loaf in my hand and the clay pot filled with beans strapped above the water jug on my back. Joas carried the sack of grain.

"If we stop now," he explained, "we would have to invite them to eat with us."

"It's all right," I said.

"I love those girls," said Almaz.

"You love too easily," Joas reproached her. "Desta, you must teach Almaz to be wary of strangers."

"And what about you?" I asked sharply. "Why must I do everything?"

Joas kept on walking. His steps were still long, but I thought I saw his shoulders slump slightly, perhaps from the weight of the grain. "Desta," he said to me softly, "I might not always be with you."

"What do you mean?" I asked, alarmed.

"I mean . . . I mean later. When . . . when we are in Israel. I will not always be with you, so I tell you these things to teach you what must be done for Almaz. She is too trusting. She kisses everyone."

"But they are just little girls, and Beta Yisrael."

"I know," Joas said. "I am saying, in general. Sometimes even Beta Yisrael cannot be trusted."

"What?" I was aghast. "How can you say such a thing, Joas?"

"If we eat more we will not be fighting all the time," said Almaz.

"You are right, little one," said Joas, giving her a smile and sitting down beside her at the edge of the path.

We were on a high plateau, with the empty hills and ravines all around us, the walls of the canyons scratched out by wind and time, to make patterns and different layers of color—brown, tan, ochre, red, gray, and some hillsides covered with bluish greenery we love so well.

We broke the bread and ate slowly, and I warned Almaz, "Don't eat too much of the inside. It sits heavily on the stomach."

This is true of all our *misvat,* and we usually leave the undercooked dough at the center uneaten. But this time we were so hungry that we dipped the soft bread into the beans with peppers, and in spite of ourselves the entire loaf was soon gone.

We drank from the water jug, then sat back, feeling the pleasure of being full. As we sat there I wondered, was it wrong to be so happy? I realized it was true; I was very happy. I thought of Aunt Kibret and Uncle Tekle; they seemed far away, and the only reality was we three here together. I looked at Joas, handsome and content now from the food, leaning back against a rock, his face raised to the sun. I watched Almaz as she cocked her head listening to the sound of some creature, until I followed her sharp gaze

95

to see a large lizard resting there, watching us, too. A moment later a bustard swooped down, caught the lizard in its beak. Silently we watched as the huge bird flew away with the lizard dangling from its beak, and in the next moment the lizard's abdomen had been split open, the innards were consumed, the skin left to fall to the ground.

None of us said anything.

Joas stood up. He lifted the sack of grain to his shoulder.

"We have to keep moving," Joas said. "We must catch up with Kess Haim and the others."

"Tonight starts Shabbat," I said. "What will we do?"

Joas kept on walking, but I heard him sigh deeply with indecision. "I say we continue."

"Travel on the Sabbath?" I asked.

"If we don't keep moving," said Joas, "we won't find them. I am thinking that on the Sabbath they will rest. It gives us a chance to catch up. Maybe our only chance."

We rested for a while during midday, eating some of the beans. By then I was sorry for having eaten the soft inner bread dough, for it lay like a stone on my stomach, and the beans on top.

We drank from the water jug. Now it was only half full and much easier to carry, and I was grateful. But Joas said we needed to fill it, and when the beans were gone, fill the bean pot with water, too.

"As soon as we find pure water," Joas said, "you can use it to make *injera* from this grain. By day, we can make a fire and not be noticed."

"Do you know where we are going?" I asked more than once.

"We are going down," Joas replied, his mouth set into a stern line. "Down the mountains to meet the others. Any more questions?"

"No."

Before dusk, I thought, we would find them. We would see the smoke from their cooking fire. Or at night. They would be chanting prayers. Surely we would hear them, even from far away. Joas is a good tracker, with sharp senses. And they would be looking for us, too. Yes, by tonight we would find them.

But night came, and still we three were alone in the vast open spaces, and now the footpath disappeared, and we made our way through thick brambles, then down again, down the sides of a steep plateau, such plateaus as are both the beauty and the curse of Ethiopia.

As the sun sank down complete, Joas stopped at last.

"We will pray," he said.

The three of us stood facing as he did, though I don't think Joas knew either which direction was east, facing Jerusalem. Still we followed him and prayed our Sabbath prayers, ate the last of the beans and then continued to walk down, down and into a deep hollow from which, suddenly, we realized there was no way out except to climb straight up again, and we were already exhausted.

"Joas, I have to rest," Almaz said weakly. She held her stomach. The beans.

"We can't," he said. "If you can't walk, I'll carry you."

"Carry her straight up these cliffs?" I cried. "Joas, come on. It's a sign. We are supposed to rest on Shabbat."

"You rest then," he tossed over his shoulder, scooping

up Almaz and leaving the sack of grain to me. "I am going on."

"We took a wrong turn!" I cried. "What are we doing down in this hole?"

Joas did not answer. His strides became longer, and I had to hurry to keep pace. "It is our punishment," I muttered. "For traveling on the Sabbath. We will never find the right path."

But Joas did not hear me. Thank God.

We walked all night, resting only once more, when I fell asleep immediately, and Almaz too, tucked into my arm for warmth. I think Joas slept this time; I don't know. But when daylight broke he was standing over me, and he pointed. "There's a village over there," he said. "I'm going to see if I can get some water. Give me the jug."

"We'll go with you," I said, scrambling to my feet.

Almaz was wide awake stretching, then holding her stomach.

"No. You both wait here. Prepare a small fire. We have to prepare *injera*. We cannot keep walking with this sack of grain, and we need food."

I hesitated. "I have no matches."

From the pack on his back Joas took a box of matches and handed them to me. "Don't waste any," he said, and with that he picked up the nearly empty water jug and disappeared.

"Get some rocks," I told Almaz.

Together we found flat stones and arranged them in a circle. We tore dried twigs from the bushes, tied them tight to give more heat to the burning.

"Are you really going to make a fire?" Almaz asked, her eyes upon me, very large, very round. At home we extinguish our fires before sunset on Friday night, and they are never rekindled until Saturday night, and always with proper Habdalah ceremony. In my whole life I have never seen anyone strike a match on the Sabbath.

"I suppose I must do it, Almaz. We have to eat."

Almaz only looked at me.

"How will Joas get water? What if the creek is guarded?"

I only shrugged. "Maybe the people are still sleeping."

"How can you make *injera* without a pan?"

"I brought a small pan," I told Almaz and took it from my pack to show her, feeling wicked to be touching it even.

Soon Joas returned, carrying the water jug high on his shoulder. Usually women carry water. Joas had a funny look on his face, as if it shamed him.

Into the empty bean pot he poured some of the water, then sat back on his heels to watch while I mixed in the *teff*, also using the sour starter the mother of those three little girls had thought to send along. Soon I had a smooth dough.

"Why haven't you started the fire?" Joas chided.

Wordless, I handed him the match.

Joas looked at me, his lips puffed outward, resolute. "Making fire is woman's work," he said, his arms folded across his chest. "Do it, Desta."

"No!"

"*Do it.*"

I half closed my eyes as I struck the match on the side of the box. It flared, and for an instant, I thought the flames would consume me. But they caught immediately on the

99

dry twigs, and now Almaz fed in the dried animal dung she had found, and Joas added a bit of wood he had brought from the creek, still damp and smouldering badly.

We laid the pan onto the rocks, and I poured out the dough, setting on the round lid to make the bread bubble.

I sat back on my heels, with a heavy feeling like a stone in my throat, and I thought, well, we are still alive. Not struck dead yet by God's thunderbolt. I was amazed and nervous and ready to cry, until in a short time my *injera* was done, and as we ate I felt only relief.

Three times more I made dough and baked it, until the sack of *teff* was empty and a stack of *injera* cakes lay beside us on the rock, ready to take on our journey. And I thought of the teaching of our people: It is impossible to break only one commandment.

We had already broken the commandment about keeping the Sabbath not once, but three times, first by traveling, then by lighting a fire, and then by baking bread. Each time it had become easier, until as I baked the final batch of *injera* and cleaned the pan with sand, I felt only a slight flush on my cheeks, no longer that deep burning shame and terror of God's vengeance. I did not look at Joas, and he avoided my eyes, too.

Three days passed and still we walked, then realized we had been wandering in a circle back to the same plateau from which we had started. We set out again, met an unpassable ravine, and understood why it is that people hire a guide to move down from these mountains.

"We are lost," Almaz said once.

"Don't say that word again," I whispered to her, clutching her hand. She had started out singing to herself. Now she was only tired, with little strength for songs, though I heard her chanting under her breath, keeping a rhythm for her steps.

Joas spoke little. His face was creased into a perpetual squint, as he sought a trail, scanned the bushes for movement, hopefully looked skyward for some signs of our friends—the flight of a buzzard to lead us to an encampment, smoke from a cooking fire, or dust from other travelers.

"Where are they? What could have happened?" I thought the questions constantly, asked only once, for the scowl on Joas's face when he replied.

"There are a thousand trails in these mountains. We can move only down, south and west, hoping to find them. Eventually we will surely come to a river where the paths meet."

I wondered, did Joas really know this? Or was he just hoping?

I knew he was worried, plenty. The problem was this: If we traveled by night, which was safer, the road was hard to see. If we traveled by day, there were the *shifta*, bandits to worry about, and soldiers, and even villagers along the way who might come out to do us harm. Amharic people do not want Falashas near their villages. They fear we will step on their grass; they think we will poison their water with our evil eye. They would catch us and beat us, the way the children beat Gennet's little brother.

We were careful to make a wide circle around any villages, going past them only at night, and then to the shrill barking of dogs, with sometimes a dog rushing out at us. One night a large yellow dog came out at us, fangs showing. Joas struck the dog on the neck with his rifle. The beast fell, legs stiff in the air. Maybe it was dead. Almaz cried out. But we had no time for pity. The villagers were aroused, and we ran and ran until we dropped by the roadside, then crept into a hollow where we could hide, and finally we slept.

Sometimes Joas carried Almaz on his back, making a game of it. Usually she walked, always some paces behind me. As she walked she chanted under her breath, over and over, "Walking to Jerusalem, walking, walking. Walking to Jerusalem we are."

My feet were tough on the bottom, hard from walking without sandals, but thorns had cut into the side of my foot, and after the bleeding stopped a scab formed and the edges began oozing with pus, but we had no time to worry about that. Almaz was looking pinched and worn out.

Joas found water in a pond, thinking it was clear. We drank from it, also filling the jug. That same day while Joas and I slept, Almaz kept running to the bushes, and I heard her groan.

"We have to get some food," Joas said. "In the next village I will get some." We had eaten the last cake of *injera* that day. Hunger was with us always, worse when we stopped walking.

"How can you?" I asked.

"I will buy it," he said.

"Will you need my coins?" I started to untie my bundle.

Joas hesitated. "No. You'd better save yours. I have some."

"I want to go with you," Almaz said. "I want to see the people."

"No," Joas said sharply. "You two wait here. If I go alone, maybe they will think I am a soldier, lost from my group."

He took up his rifle, leaving his pack with us, but wearing his *shamma*.

It was some minutes before I realized that I sat quite alone among the shrubbery. I called softly to Almaz. No answer.

I called again, looking through the bushes. No Almaz.

Slowly I set out in an ever-widening circle, as Joas had taught me, keeping the center of our small encampment always in mind and in view. There is a trick to finding landmarks; it takes a good eye and memory. Circling, at last I came upon Almaz crouched in the scooped-out trunk of a tree which lay on its side surrounded by rocks and mounds of earth, a cozy nest.

"Almaz!" I breathed. "What are you doing?"

She pointed. We were just above a village, looking down upon the tops of *tukels*. We could see the field of chick-peas, empty, for it was early still, and not harvest season in any case. A few women were about, fetching water early, mixing grain for *injera*. A shepherd boy came out of a *tukel* and disappeared around a lean-to, then emerged with a tiny goat in his arms.

"Sweet!" murmured Almaz.

Then we saw Joas. With his gun ready in his right hand, he ran swiftly to the side of a *tukel*, then disappeared into the storage shed.

Beside me Almaz was breathing heavily.

Far below us several chickens fluttered their wings in warning. From the *tukel* a girl emerged, her face nearly covered with her *shamma,* carrying a basket, looking for eggs.

Unwittingly, I gasped. *Joas!*

Joas came out of the shed, rifle in one hand, his *shamma* bulging under his other arm, full of booty.

The girl saw him, and before she could scream, I saw Joas lift the rifle.

The girl froze.

Joas spoke to her. I could see the threat in his posture and the fear in hers. He put the rifle to her chest, held the barrel there for a long, terrible moment. The moment lasted; I had the feeling of great heat, as if something here would burn us alive.

The next moment Joas had lowered the rifle and was running, then disappeared from view. The girl screamed.

Almaz and I ran back to the encampment.

When Joas came to us, he was breathless and coughing.

I could not look at him without seeing a man, a soldier with a rifle raised, ready to kill—it was the way that girl saw him. And yet, he was my brother.

Almaz and I kept quiet, looking down. Joas motioned to us to follow him away from this place. We did.

Much later, as I mixed the stolen grain with water and roasted the three eggs Joas had brought, I thought again of our saying: It is impossible to break only one commandment.

9

WE KNEW BY THE SETTING AND THE RISING SUN THAT WE were going in the right direction; first south out of the high plateaus, then we would have to turn westward into Sudan.

Days passed in a blur—five, six, seven. At first we were climbing ever downward, clinging to the rocks and cliffs, amazed when we looked back to see how far and how steeply we had come, how the magical shapes of rocks and crags played in our minds, so that we imagined tall *tukels* and towers and giants among us.

As we descended the vegetation changed, grew thick and tangled, with sharp ravines still dividing the land, then the ground rolling beneath us, studded with rocks, crested with shrubs behind which hid the shy creatures of the land. An occasional creek, too, teemed with life: Frogs and toads, lizards, green snakes, and crocodiles whose teeth did gleam so in the moonlight! We no longer minded the dark. Instead, daylight seemed now too bright, beaming into our eyes too strongly.

Part of the night was its sounds, jackals and hyenas, birds and monkeys. We heard the roar of leopards, lions, and wild dogs in the distance. I felt no fear of the animals, only of man.

It seemed that we were becoming like the animals. Our life took on a different rhythm. We slept on the ground, we foraged for food, we searched for signs of water, and we walked.

Joas only half slept, guarding Almaz and me with the rifle. Day and night he searched for our friends.

On the sixth day we met a trader carrying a load of skins on his back. Joas asked whether he had seen a small caravan of ten or twelve people, some mules, and an old woman on a litter. The trader nodded, showing a mouthful of golden teeth. "Passed them over a day ago!" the man said. "Keep on, you'll find them." We walked faster, on into the daylight. Our rest was sparse, merely four hours, then Joas pulled us to our feet again, and we walked all night until dawn, at last settling down. We had neither food nor water, but I was so tired that I forgot my hunger for once and prepared to sleep deeply.

"I'm going on ahead," said Joas. "You two rest here. I'll come back for you."

"But where are you going?" I cried. "Why would you leave us?"

"They must be close now," Joas said. "If we keep resting, we'll never catch up. The trader said he had passed them."

"Maybe he lied," I said.

Joas faced me, shocked. "Why would he lie?"

"He saw your rifle. Maybe he told you what you wanted to hear."

Joas blew out his breath, and he wavered. Then firmly he said, "I'm going to find them." He stood with his hand raised to shield his eyes, searching the horizon. "Look."

"What?" I said crossly. "I don't see anything."

"There, there—far beyond the rocks, down by the clumps of trees, rising from that gully, don't you see it? Smoke. Smoke! That means a campfire."

Joas bent down, searching the ground for signs, murmuring to himself as he moved off the trail and back again. "Hoofprints," he said. "Droppings. Surely some mules and people passing by in a group all together. A broken pot there in the bushes. Someone has camped here not long ago. It must be them. It must!"

In that moment I realized, by the joy in Joas's voice, how great the burden had been for him, how desperately he wanted the others.

I, too, was suddenly filled with joyful strength. How happy I would be to see Dan and Kess Haim and old Weizero Channa and the others from our village!

"Let us come with you!" I begged. "Please, Joas."

"No. You wait here. Rest—you said you were tired. From the distance of that fire, I should be able to return to you soon. I will bring a mule back for you to ride! Come now, don't argue for once."

"Kess! Weizero Channa!" Almaz shrieked, jumping up and down. "It is smoke, let us come with you, Joas!"

Joas seemed about to relent, then he shook his head. "No. I want you two to wait here. Don't leave this place, I say it! I will bring back food and a mule for you to ride, Almaz. Just don't leave here."

Joas moistened his hands with water from the jug, wiped

the dust from his face, and picked up the rifle.

Almaz and I settled down to wait. I suppose we slept a little, but my heart was racing so with the need to be reunited with our people that I woke with a start and saw Almaz beside me braiding some grass, and I heard her singing softly.

Almaz knows every song I have ever heard. We sang together then, keeping time with our hands, and then we lay back letting the sun touch our faces. It was warm. Lower now from the high plateaus, the weather was changing, and we put off our *shammas* and sat under a bit of shade from several large bushes.

"He said it was not far," Almaz said after a time. "I thought he would be back by now, and with a mule and some food."

"Maybe he is talking to them. We'll go a short way and look," I said.

We took up our bundles and moved out slowly, until we came to a mound from which we could see all around. Below us lay one last row of cliffs, and then as far as the eye could scan, valleys and meadows, a gully and below that, thick tangled masses of green. Just before the gully I could see the smoke that had attracted Joas; it was an encampment. Faint traces of dust rose from it.

"It's them!" Almaz said. "Their camp. Let's go."

"Quiet. We're to wait for Joas." I wanted to feel the joy that shone in Almaz's eyes; somehow I could not. I felt only a strange sense of suspicion and fear.

I stood up, scanning the ledge, then looking beyond to lower ground I saw a white spot in the distance, moving, jumping between shadows and shrubs, the spot getting closer, until I could make out Joas's shape as he climbed the jagged boulders toward the ledge. He came up surefooted, one hand down on the rocks, his *shamma* bright in the sun. I saw him straighten as he reached the top, and he stood with his hand shading his eyes.

A shot rang out. Sudden and shattering, it left an echo. Joas fell.

I turned to Almaz, saw her wild look, and swiftly I caught her, put my hand over her mouth, pulled her down with me behind a thick screen of bushes, and held her there trembling, my fingers clenched so tight around her arms that they ached.

"Don't move," I whispered once.

We crouched motionless. I could feel my heart pounding in my chest and throat, my eyes aching from trying to see through the shrubs; some knowledge—or was it training from Joas?—told me that we must not move, that whoever had shot Joas would come looking for other travelers, and if they found us, two girls alone . . .

We waited and waited, and at last heard them; the scraping steps of men's sandals, jovial shouts at their discovery. Their voices rang out clear, echoing among the rocks, though they were still a good distance away.

"Got him clean! A fine shot."

"Ha! He won't need that rifle anymore."

"Look into his pockets. Maybe he carries plenty of bullets."

"A handful only!" I heard a muffled sound, a kick against unresisting flesh.

Beside me I felt Almaz trembling; her teeth chattered.

I stared at her. She put her hands over her mouth.

"Doesn't he have any money?"

"A few coins," came the voice, sullen. "Hardly worth the effort of climbing up here."

"Well, take his pants and coat, at least. We can use them. The shirt is no good, thanks to your bullet hole."

"I could use that *shamma*."

"Take it, you old buzzard. It stinks. *Zah*, who wants the old thing?"

Through all this, while I heard the words, my mind went blank, like an empty vessel, ringing, ringing, the way an empty water jug sounds when a finger is snapped against it.

"Where is his mule?"

"The fool was on foot."

"Alone? Is it possible?"

"Well, if he was hunting . . ."

"What is that around his neck? Let me see it. Look, you, I found it first."

Sounds. Tearing. Panting sounds of men in earnest about what they want.

"Take it then. It's not worth a *burr*. Only an old bead."

"And useless, too," said another, laughing. "It did little to protect *him*."

I thought of Joas's amulet, the bead he always wore close against that hollow in his throat. Still my head rang, and all I could see was a haze between the bushes, and that last vision of Joas standing on the ledge looking all around. He had come up to warn us, was looking for us surely, to warn us to be quiet, to make no fire. He must have crept near enough to know they were *shifta*, then soundlessly turned to leave them—and then when he reached the high place, they saw him and swiftly took aim.

"Maybe he had a wife." Laughter.

"We could search here, maybe find her."

"It is getting late. You want to be up here in the dark? We should take on some water, then be off."

"I would not mind having a woman."

"You?" Laughter. "What would you do with a woman, old goat?"

"Ha, I would show you."

We heard the scraping of their feet; from far away, we heard the whinnying of a horse.

"Sounds as if somebody is getting at the animals."

"Fool! I said one of us should stay there to guard them!"

A shot rang out. It echoed with a strange sound, having hit rock. Their voices faded; soon all was silent, and from the distance again we heard the horses, then nothing more.

For a long while Almaz and I remained there, motionless.

At last I crept out from our hiding place, and I saw that the sun was low in the horizon, and I blinked at the knowledge that it was late afternoon; we had lain there for hours, trembling. My legs were cramped and weak. I lay down on my belly, to gaze to the place where the bandits had been camped. Nothing.

"They are gone," I said aloud.

Almaz came forth, crawling on her knees.

"Get up. They are gone."

She shook her head, crouched there like an animal.

"I have to go down there," I said, breathing heavily. "To the rocks. You wait here."

"No," said Almaz. Her features were firm. "I don't stay alone. Never."

I sighed and took her hand.

Slowly and carefully we made our way down to the rock formations, to the flat place where we had last seen Joas standing with his hand shading his eyes.

His body was stretched out on its side, as if he were sleeping, arms out. They had taken his pants, sandals, and *shamma*. It was this, the sight of my brother's bare legs, that caught me like an iron weight around the chest, a weight of hatred such as I have never felt before, bringing a red rage pounding in my head, rage enough to take my Uncle Tekle's iron hammer and beat them dead.

I had seen people dead before, but not like this. Not out in the wilderness, alone, and with darkness coming, lying stiff and cold, and the wind starting to moan through the rocks, and sobs coming from somewhere, not the loud wailing funeral cries, but a steady soft sobbing, like whispers of grief seeping out of all the corners and cracks of the earth.

My head felt strangely light, my arms heavy as stones as I bent down and lifted my brother's head. It rolled back, heavy. His lips were parted, his eyes half-open. Now I could see a single small hole had cut cleanly through his back. Just a single small hole, with blood around it in a circle, turning dark.

I touched his hand, the dark fingers, stroking them one by one, feeling the stiffness there, thinking strange thoughts, that if I rubbed his hands, only rubbed them long enough, life would return.

"Don't." From Almaz, a single, heartrending cry.

I turned to stare at her, startled. I had felt myself quite alone, alone with the whispering sobs. Now I realized it was she who was sobbing so quietly, her hands over her mouth, her body wracked back and forth, back and forth.

Still, I could not go to her. I felt frozen, unable to move, unable to hold her warmth and life against me, when my brother lay here on the rocks, stiff and cold.

"Almaz," I said, in a voice that was new to me, "I want you to go back to where we were hiding. Bring our bundles. Bring my holiday *shamma*."

Almaz looked at me. She was doubled over, her eyes swollen.

"Do it," I said.

Without a word she crept away, and some time later she returned with our things.

"Here."

I took my bundle and pulled out the *shamma*, and I laid it on top of Joas. Then, straining and panting, I moved him a little, then back, then again to the other side, until the *shamma* was wrapped around him and my face was layered with sweat, though it was getting dark now and cool.

I sat hunched beside my brother's body for a long time, and Almaz beside me. The moon came up, bright. It lighted the rocks; it shone on my holiday *shamma*. We swayed silently; I realized then that we were praying.

"We have to bury him," I said.

"How?"

"I . . . ." I gazed up at the sky, at the moon and stars. How? I had been to burials before, but always with someone in charge, the *kess* and the elders offering prayers and ceremonies, someone having dug a grave, many hands to help bring stones, an old woman to wash the corpse with reverence, then to wrap it in a clean, new shroud; the mourners, the wailers, the ones who bring food—where were they?

I swallowed down the great knot in my throat. A sound came from my lips. I looked up again at the sky. A long trail of stars seemed to form an arc, pointing somewhere, somewhere.

Down on all fours now I slipped across the rocks, searching for a place where the soil was not too hard, where the space might be sheltered by a ledge from above, and all I could think of was this: God, grant me a place, a grave. God, grant me a place for my brother.

It was there, as if He had prepared it and guided me now.

I climbed back up to Almaz.

"Give me your *shamma*," I said.

"What for?"

"To wrap his head. I'll give it back to you after—after we get him down the rocks. I found a place. We can dig it out a little."

We managed. It was hard to be gentle. But we got him down the rocks, down to the place where there was a pocket of soil with a low ledge overhanging it, and nearby a small tree. In the distance we could hear the rush of a stream.

I found a stone, jagged and sharp, and with this I began to scrape away the soil, scraping and scraping in the same motion endlessly. I became aware of Almaz beside me, doing the same, until my fingers ached and my back seemed forever bent, and the sky was fading from black to dusky gray in that time just before morning.

We heard the snapping of a branch.

A family of ibex, mother and two babies, stared at us with wide eyes, then bolted down to the clearing where the bandits had been camped.

"Water," said Almaz.

"Yes. We will drink later."

We could not lift Joas. Carefully we dragged him to the grave, too shallow, but it was all we could do.

I took Almaz's *shamma* from his head, handed it back to her, then covered his face gently with the end of my holiday *shamma*.

"Bring leaves," I said.

We gathered them, laid them over him.

"What is the prayer?" Almaz whispered.

I shook my head, could think of no other words but these: "Hear, O Israel, the Lord is our God, the Lord is One. Blessed is the Lord."

"He gives life," said Almaz.

"Yes," I replied. I began to gather stones.

Almaz too.

We laid them on top, a thick mound, enough to keep him free from preying beasts or birds.

Wordless, Almaz and I walked down and found the stream. Cold as it was in early morning, we knelt down and washed our heads, our hands, then our feet, until our bodies were numb with chill, our teeth chattering.

Still numb, we found a space beyond the stream, spread the skin over us tight, and we slept.

10

ALL MY LIFE I HAD BEEN A CHILD. ALWAYS THERE HAD BEEN someone to tell me what to do, to show me where to go. Now there was nobody. And I had Almaz.

Grief does strange things to the body. When we woke up my mind was empty at first. Suddenly I remembered, and the words hit me like blows—my brother is dead. The words repeated and repeated; still I could not think of it truly. Dead? No, no, if we wait for a while, wash our faces and hands, he will appear from around the tree; he just went ahead to scout for us, or to find food. Soon Joas will come, and he will scold me for not having made the fire, or for something. He will be cross with me; he will remind me to check the water; he will tell me to keep out of sight. . . .

Another part of me stood by, nearly laughing: You fool. Joas will tell you nothing anymore. He is dead.

"What are we going to do?"

Almaz, having awakened, came to me, her face looking swollen.

"We will wash our faces," I said. My tone was heavy, flat. "Are you hungry?"

"No."

I had no wish for food either. It was as if my body had left me; it had no desires at all, only to sleep and forget.

After we washed we did see an inset tree, and we gathered the false banana.

"Eat," I told Almaz, peeling the fruit, holding it out to her.

"I can't, Desta. Please, don't force me."

Almost gagging, I ate. I had to keep up my strength and to set an example for Almaz. Somehow, I was able to hold it down.

"What are we going to do?" Almaz repeated.

My mind clouded over. I gazed out at the land; behind us lay the steep rocky cliffs, the plateau, the mountains from which we had come. Perhaps we could rest here, then begin the long upward climb, find the paths we had taken, somehow retrace our footsteps, and go back home. Home. The word was like a precious ointment laid over a raw wound. Home. What must they be doing now? Did Aunt Kibret miss us? Home.

"We are going to go over to those bushes," I said, pointing. "There is a small waterfall. See that little glade with all the leaves? We are going to wait there until it is cooler. Then we are going to go . . ." I stood up, squinting to the distance, seeing that the land dipped down, gradually down, to a thick, tangled belt of greenery. "We are going to go that way. You see, the sun is before us. We must go that way. West."

"We are not going back? We are not going home?"

"Almaz, we are going home," I said. "Home to Jerusalem."

We waited, screened by the shrubbery. Suddenly it seemed there was nothing to do. With Joas, there had always been a plan, some kind of talk, even laughter. Now, silence held us; we sat and watched birds coming to sip from the pond. We saw lizards and toads and small water snakes wriggling, snapping up insects for food, staying alive.

Almaz slept, twitching, crying out. When she awakened she looked at me, her eyes deep and hollow, torn between trust and doubt. "Desta?" She spoke only my name, but the way she said it meant much more.

"Yes. I'm here. Listen, I want to tell you a story."

"A story?" Almaz sighed and rubbed her eyes. I could see her chest heave and the misery in her eyes. I knew exactly how she felt.

"Yes. A story. When we get to Jerusalem, you must know some stories to tell your new friends. You don't want them to think you are ignorant! They will say to you, 'Little black girl, tell us, where did you come from?' "

Almaz smiled, nearly laughing at the way I said "little black girl." Talk about color always makes her laugh.

"So, you will say to them, 'Listen: Long ago, when Solomon was king of the Jews in Jerusalem, he wanted to build his temple, and he sent for peoples from all over the world to bring him treasures.' "

"Why would they come to him?" asked Almaz, still rubbing her eyes.

"Because he was very wise," I said. "Everyone had heard

of him. Also, he had copper, plenty, to trade."

"What is copper?"

"Copper is . . . copper is copper," I said. "Listen. So the queen, Makeda . . ."

"The Queen of Sheba," put in Almaz, listening now.

"Yes, Makeda of Sheba decided to go and visit this famous wise king. She brought him spices, plenty, and gold from Ethiopia, coming in a large caravan laden with precious things. She journeyed far—just as far as we are going now. Exactly as far," I said, amazed and impressed with the idea for the first time, thinking: *This very journey has been done before, by Queen Makeda! Surely we can do it too.*

"Of course," I said, "it was easier for the queen. She had camels and probably a coach. But still . . ."

"Are we going the same route she did?" Almaz asked, interested now.

"I don't know. I don't think so. But our destination is the same. So be quiet. Listen. This queen was very beautiful, you know. *I* always think she looked something like Aunt Kibret."

"Aunt Kibret is very beautiful," Almaz said. "Especially in her holiday clothes."

"Yes. Well, the queen came to Solomon, and of course he fell in love with her. He wanted to sleep with her. She said no, she would not, because they were not married, you see."

"Why did he want to sleep with her?"

"Because he liked her, and because he wanted her to have his son. Well, she said she would not sleep in his bed, and he said all right, but she had to agree not to take anything of his in the night, or else she would have to sleep with him."

"Why did he want to sleep with her?" Almaz asked again, innocent.

"Almaz, I told you. Because he wanted to have a child with her. Sleeping together means—well, it means they lie together very close, and that is how babies are made. Don't you know anything?"

"I guess not. Well, go on. Did she sleep with him or not?"

"Yes, she did. Solomon was very wise, but he was also tricky. He gave her very much pepper and spice to eat for supper, so that Makeda got very thirsty in the night, and got up to take some water. Well, the water did not belong to her, did it? King Solomon caught her taking the water, and he said, 'Aha! you have not kept your word. Now the forfeit is mine!' So he got into her bed and did sleep with her, and when she was ready to leave Jerusalem she was carrying his son."

"Where?"

"In her belly, that's where. You know this, Almaz. You are only pretending to be so dumb. Well, the queen went back home to Ethiopia with gifts from Solomon, including some good leaders from his army going to help her on the journey and to set up a fine kingdom."

"Did they build the palaces?"

"Yes. Of course. Back in Ethiopia, they built fine palaces, and of course, they had brought with them Torah. So when Makeda got back, she began to keep the commandments and to worship God, the way we still do today."

"What about Menelik? The son?"

"You tell it," I said.

"The son wanted to go back to Jerusalem to see his father, King Solomon. And he did. And Solomon blessed him and said, you are the king of the Jewish nation in Ethiopia."

"Yes. And so, now these many years later, we are still his descendants, going home now at last, to Jerusalem."

"Is the story true?"

"Yes. Even the Christians and Muslims tell it; only the Christians changed after a time, following Jesus."

"Why didn't we change, too?"

"We liked the old ways," I said. "They felt good to us, and true."

"Desta," she said softly, her voice trembling. "I miss Joas."

I sighed. "So do I." I stood up, looked carefully around. "We must get water, as much as we can carry," I said. "Then we will start."

"How do we know which way to go?"

"We will go down. To that green place. Joas said there would be a jungle. Every morning we will walk, so we will know the sun is in our back. Then we will rest when it is hottest. Later, we will walk again so that the sun is in our eyes. That will be the right way to go."

Almaz nodded. "Good."

"And we'll look for smoke and tracks. We'll find Kess Haim and the others. When we walk, we have to watch for footprints and signs."

"Do you know how to do that, Desta?"

"Oh, yes," I said. My heart leaped in my throat—lies always do this to me.

"We have to find some food, Almaz," I said. "We must find a village."

"And steal food?"

I shook my head. "No. We will buy it. I can trade my necklace."

We set out. Walking with Joas was one thing; I had only to keep my eyes upon his back and to put one foot in front of the other. If we came to a ravine too steep or a cliff to high to scale down, we turned around, and the blame was his, also the decision. Now I kept remembering my own words to Almaz, about the sun, following the sun. Joas had been able to keep his mind on directions, so we walked at night. I knew I would not be able to do this; I needed the sun to show me. So we would walk by day, taking chances. There was no other way.

All the rest of the day we walked, and at night we slept. The water was good for our thirst, and we found more at a small flowing creek. But hunger started to come to us now, and I saw no villages, nothing but earth and brush and a vastness that scared me, plenty.

The next day my mouth felt very dry, my tongue swollen, even though I drank. Almaz began to heave. Nothing came out from her; no food was in her, only the water, and that should not be lost either.

Small paths twisted and turned, some made by animals, others by human feet. It was hard to know the difference. Small paths could lead to water, to caves, to villages with good people or to evil. How could I know which?

Well, we knew that villages are set up by water, usually on a high place, so people can look down at who is coming and be prepared. Villages are set onto flat spaces, so that fields can be plowed and crops grow; but everything here was hilly and even the trees were different and the birds, too, with different feathers and looking at us, curious, as if we did not belong.

It was nearly evening of the second day, and my mouth felt too strange. I kept swallowing, then up would come sour spit, and wide empty yawning of my stomach, again and again.

"We have to eat," I muttered.

To the next narrow path I set my feet, no longer caring where the sun was, looking for only one thing: food.

We curved and climbed, climbed and turned. Thick trees blotted out light, and I heard the sounds of screeching. Birds. Birds flew in and out of trees, swooping low, and I thought, yes, they are doing the same thing as we, finding food in a village, where there are people.

We crept closer. And now, joy, we found two things— not only was there a village above us, with *tukels* and pasture, but at the side we could see a road, not the slim foot trails we had been seeking, but a real road worn wide by feet and animals and even carts.

"A road! Praise God!" I gasped out to Almaz. "Come, first we have to go to the village to get some food."

I looked at Almaz, straightened her *shamma*, smoothed down her hair. Still, she had a wild look.

"How do I look?" I asked.

"All right," she said. "In truth? Terrible."

123

I wiped my face with my *shamma,* moistened my lips and tried to smile. A smile would be nice, I thought, for meeting people, asking to buy food. Somehow, I could not make a smile come to me.

We moved up, up, walking slowly, holding ourselves proud. "Don't slouch," I told Almaz. "Keep your head up. We are not thieves."

In my hand I held the blue beads from my mother. In such villages beads are better for trading than coin, for how can these people spend money? I knew how to bargain. I had seen it done often enough. And my jewels had value.

Of course they saw us coming, and a few children gathered to stare at us, dirty and ragged and noses running.

"Hello!" we said, pleasant and kind, "What news? We are just traveling, so, and stopping here to see you."

None of the children said a word, but only looked at us with big eyes, with fingers stuck into their noses and mouths.

A man came, hurrying, with a rifle in his hand. He shouted to the children, "Be gone!" and they scattered like frightened hens. "What is it you want?" he said to us, scowling, a lean man, his face withered from years and from anger.

"We thought . . . we are travelers," I said, my voice low, eyes down. "Our brother is below there, gathering fuel."

"Why does he send you here? What sort of girls are you?"

My heart pounded.

"If you could spare some grain, perhaps," I said, my voice coming out like a faint wind, wavering, "some vegetables."

"You are Falashas, aren't you," the man said. He leaned

toward us, his eyes narrowed. "Get out of this place. Out!"

"We can pay you," I whispered, desperate, my throat so very dry, my tongue thick.

"Don't you hear me? Get out, I say! We don't want your filthy money. You're lucky I don't kill you, but let you leave here with all your limbs whole. We don't want your kind on our land, don't you hear it?"

A stone came flying, swift, against my cheek. Another hit the side of my eye. The children had climbed onto a roof. The stones were sharp, flying, the children squealing as they threw them, their mouths wide open now as they panted with excitement.

We ran, I dragging Almaz, but not fast enough. A large rock hit her head. Blood spurted out.

The road, the road, the road, I thought, pulling Almaz behind me, and once she fell, skidded along the ground, her legs scraping so, but I shouted at her, "Come on, run, run!" until I realized we had left them far behind and I was pulling poor Almaz without mercy.

We lay, panting, amid a pile of twigs that somebody had dropped from a load sometime.

I looked at Almaz. She had wrapped her *shamma* around her head. It was blood-stained and filthy.

I pressed the cloth more firmly against the wound.

"Are you all right?"

She nodded.

I don't know how long we sat with nothing in sight, nothing to hope for. "Get up," I said at last.

"I'm too tired."

"Get up."

Every step was painful, heavy. I needed some words to

move me. Walking, walking, I whispered to myself, walking to Jerusalem . . . we are.

"Look!" Almaz suddenly said, pointing.

There to the side of the road something fluttered with color. Someone had hung a cloth between branches to make a shelter of sorts.

"Stay here," I said softly.

"No. I don't stay alone. Never."

"All right. Come with me."

We walked softly, carefully, to spy on them first, but with the next turn we stood face to face with these people, four of them, a woman, a man, and two children. Muslims, as we could see from the clothes of the man and woman. The children were naked, entirely. The man wore a headcloth, but his robe was in rags. The woman was pregnant, plenty, her belly full and tight, and she too was in rags, and her arms like thin sticks, the eyes too hollow, too awful.

At our approach the man started. They had nothing, no packs, not even a water jug, not even a rusted old can for water. The children squatted beside their father, silent, their eyes strangely glazed.

"Peace to you," I said softly. "What news?"

"Peace to you," said the woman, a soft, musical voice, but faint from exhaustion.

"We are travelers," I said, taking Almaz close to me. "On our way down the mountains."

"We too," said the man. "But our strength fails us now without food these many days."

One of the children stood up. His legs were like sticks, his belly rounded.

I motioned with my head. "Behind us there is a village,"

I said. "There was a storehouse, perhaps some grain."

"Allah does not want us to steal," said the man.

"I have blue beads from town," I said. I had them still in my hand from before. Now I opened my hand to show him. "If you take these beads and go to the village, maybe they will trade you some food. We could share it."

The woman blinked at me. Her eyes, so large and beautiful, seemed to shine. "Allah has sent you," she whispered.

"You will give us this treasure?" asked the man.

"To share," I said. "We can wait here. With your children and wife."

"Do you have water?"

"A little," I said.

He reached out.

Wordless, I gave him the jug and he drank, only one swallow. Then he gave it back.

"Now I can go," he said.

He stood up, his rags barely covering him, but he smiled slightly, and carried himself as if he were dressed in linen.

"I'll come back soon," he said to his wife. "Just wait here with these good children. I'll come back soon."

We sat down with the woman and the children.

"Where are you from?" she asked me faintly.

"From the mountains," I replied.

She nodded. To ask questions is not too polite, or too safe.

"We are from the north," she said with a sigh. "We were told there is a feeding station to the south of here. For people like us, whose land is useless now. There were more of us, but my little girl got sick, and they would not wait."

"She is sick?" I asked, looking at the naked little girl now staring at us.

"Oh, no. Not this one. The sick one died."

Almaz moved closer to the little girl. I glanced at the mother. She nodded slightly, yes.

Almaz reached out, touched the child's cheek, then her hands, crooning, "Hello, little girl, I am Almaz. What is your name? Do you want some water? Here—a sip. That's good, isn't it?"

"What is a feeding station?" I asked.

"It is a—a place to get food. There is a country that gives it. Called the Red Cross."

"Where is that country?" I asked.

She shrugged. "I don't know. I only know they built a station where there is food and medicine. For people like us. So we go there. If we have the strength."

I wondered, then what? Where would they go after they had been fed? I did not dare to ask the desperate woman, but only tried to smile at her, as if there were no such worries.

The man came back soon with a stack of *injera* cakes and some turnips, still black from the garden, and a small jug of *tella*.

I have never had a better meal than that one we shared with the Muslim family.

After the meal they nodded to us, and they asked, "Will you walk with us? To the Red Cross?"

"No," I replied. "We must go west, to the setting sun."

"Then go with the love of Allah," they said. "And peace be with you."

11

THE ROAD FILLING WITH PEOPLE, WOMEN WITH EGGS AND VEGetables to sell, baskets on their heads and hips, men with goats straggling and bleating, all showed we were nearing a town on market day. Oh, glory! To get lost among the others, maybe to use a few coins to buy something, unnoticed as Beta Yisrael. We had to take a chance.

I looked closely at Almaz. "You do not look like a Jew," I said. I wiped her face clean, pulled her torn *shamma* close around her.

"Neither do you," she said, laughing.

For a moment I had the strong thought: If I were to take a coal and rub it hard on Almaz's forehead in the sign of a cross . . .

"We will be very quiet," I said. "Walk softly. Do not greet anyone, and don't talk to animals!" Almaz has this way of bending down to little creatures, and she must not attract notice. I prayed that nobody from that evil village would be there or recognize us. In any case, I pulled my *shamma* close over my face, as the Muslim women do, and we went following the others to the town.

We had just gotten to the edge of it, with small stalls there all around, people sitting in the center the way they do, gossiping, and Almaz clinging to my hand while we looked and looked, trying to figure out who was peaceful and who was bad, not having much luck with faces, when suddenly a hand came on my shoulder, and I jumped, whirling, straight then looking into the face of Melake, Dan's second cousin.

"Melake!" It was not a shout, but a gasp, and we clasped each other hard, we three, weeping with joy and surprise.

"Desta! Desta! We have been searching for you and today I said to Weizero, maybe they will be in the town for the small market, maybe, and here you are, praise God!"

Melake's face is round and friendly, always full of smiles. He smiled now, beaming and nodding, talking, talking of his gladness. He will never be a *kess* or a *shmagile*, this one, but he is full of smiles and good intentions, and that is sometimes better than wisdom.

We took in each other's faces, so joyful, and then Melake asked, "But where is Joas?"

My joy flew from me. Melake's face changed, too.

We moved far from the edge of the crowd, Melake following close, and then we three looked at each other, first only our eyes telling the story, and then words.

"*Shifta* killed Joas," I said. "Three days ago."

"What? What?" he cried, moaning deeply. "How? But I knew him—we had school together. Lord, Lord, Joas is my *zamed*, too!"

I wanted to weep with Melake; tears rolled down his face, and he dug his fists into his eyes, lashed at his hair with his fingers, shaking his head and his whole body in grief. But I could not cry. At last I told Melake everything that had happened.

"Melake," I said at last, "where is Dan? Where are Kess Haim and the others?"

"Oh, Desta." Melake sank down on the ground beside us. He wiped his face with his *shamma*. Of course, I had never spoken to Melake alone before, only when we were in a large group together with our relatives. Now, he and I were talking with only Almaz here and yet I felt no strangeness. I looked closely at Melake and saw changes in him; a tightening around his eyes, a nervous and lean look. I wondered, had changes also scratched lines into my face?

"Desta, there's so much to tell you," Melake said. "We'll go to Dan and Weizero Channa. They are waiting."

"Far away?"

"No, not far. Come."

"Should we buy some food while we are here?" I asked.

"Kasa, our guide, is there buying for us," said Melake, with a wave of his head. "It is safer that way. If you wish, I can tell him to buy for you, too."

I dug out some coins from the cloth in my pack, five *burr*.

"What will he get for this?" I asked.

Melake shrugged. "We must take what he offers."

He hurried to find Kasa, and we saw him talking, gesturing, then Melake returned to us.

"Kasa said to go ahead. He will catch up with us later. He has friends here." Melake frowned.

"You do not believe this Kasa?" I asked.

"He is a rascal. You will see. But come, we'll go to

Dan and Weizero. It's not far, an hour, two at the most. Come!"

The three of us set out, Melake leading, turning onto a road that was well worn by footsteps. Every now and then Melake gave us a look of sympathy, smiling, saying, "It's not far now. Not far." Melake was always that way, full of feeling and smiles. But then his tone became heavy as he told us everything.

"We waited for you until dark that first night," he said, "and when you did not come, the guide said we must start. He said there were soldiers on the road, he did not know which, but he could not be responsible for our safety if we did not follow him immediately."

"You said he is a rascal. How do you know he won't betray you?"

"He works for money." Melake shrugged. "We have no choice but to trust him. So we had to leave, but the *kess* said not to worry, we would find you on the road."

"Oh, Melake!" I sighed. "If only you had."

"But where were you? There is only one main road to our village from yours."

"Joas said to take the side road," I explained. "We came by way of the cliffs. Then we got lost in a ravine. It was hard without a guide and at night."

"Every day we looked for you!"

"And we for you!" Almaz assured him. "We didn't even stop for Shabbat, but kept on traveling, always hoping to catch you."

Melake said, "We never stopped for Shabbat."

I was shocked. "You traveled? And Kess allowed it?"

132

Melake turned to me. "He had no choice. The guide said it must be. We had to follow the guide."

"But where is Kess Haim now? Have they gone ahead? You said only Dan and Weizero Channa . . ."

Melake stopped. His face glistened with sweat. He pointed to a rock and we sat down. "Rest a moment. I will tell you." He wiped his face again with the edge of his *shamma*, and I saw that it was full of holes, the edge tattered. "We went with the guide. Going fast all night, and even part of the day. We had the mule for Weizero Channa, and we men taking turns with the litter. The guide knew where to find water. We gave him money, and he went to the villages to buy food for us."

"How wonderful!" I broke in.

"Not so wonderful. Sometimes he was good, when he was happy. Other times, he was angry, like an animal, walking with his head down, grumbling all the time. He had a *zar* in him, that man. From chewing *qat*, you see. When he was out of *qat*, he went looking, looking to buy it, angry and grumbling so. When he had plenty, well he chewed and chewed, and turned to talking until he laughed. You know what they say about *qat* chewers."

"Yes." Beta Yisrael do not chew, but we have seen others happy from the leaves, then half-crazy as their supply ends.

"So he was out of it one time, near noon, and heard sounds. It was traders, he said. We wanted to run to meet them, for we needed things too, grain and vegetables."

Melake stopped talking. He moistened his lips, gave me a quick glance, then looked away again.

"Well, Weizero Channa was sleeping, still on the litter,

and begged us to let her rest in the shade. Dan and I agreed to wait with her for a while, then catch up, carrying her, while the others went ahead."

Melake's forehead creased into a frown. He rubbed his hand over his eyes. Then he continued. "They went, everyone, and taking the mule, too. There was a small market on the road between two villages, and there were people, plenty, trading everything you could want, and the guide got his *qat*, and was happy again. But on the way back . . ." He took a breath, began again. "On the way back they were captured."

"Captured?" Almaz repeated the word.

"Dergue soldiers. Had seen them at the market, I suppose. That is why now we don't trade. Kasa must do it for us. The soldiers came with rifles. They hit Kess Haim. He was bleeding from his mouth and blood running from his ear. They took some of our people away. Two were girls from our village. They took the mule, too."

"Where did they take them?"

Melake shrugged. "To prison."

"And now?"

"We know nothing. They are in prison. How long they'll stay, we don't know. Whether they torture them, we don't know. They could kill them. Who would complain?"

"But how did you know what happened to them? If you and Dan and Weizero were hidden and waiting?"

"Oh. The guide told us. They arrested him, too. Maybe that was just for show. He says he bought his way out. We waited two days not knowing what to do, and he returned to us." Melake shrugged. "Who knows the truth of all this?

Maybe they will send Kess Haim and the others back to the villages."

"Sent back? Oh, Melake. No."

Melake nodded, twisting his hands. "Sometimes they send them back in such a way that they can never try to escape again. You know what I mean?"

"Yes."

Melake got up. "We must go now," he said. From his pocket he took a cake of *injera*, flat and moldy with age. He broke it into pieces, handed one to me, one to Almaz.

"Thank you, Melake."

"We have food," said Melake. "Plenty, plenty. You must eat with us. We have everything."

I looked at him, and in spite of myself I smiled. The words were pleasant to hear, though certainly false. But our people remember courtesy, always.

We walked on. "If Joas had brought us to you that night, and if we had been there on the road, we would have been captured, too," I said.

"Then Joas might still be alive," Almaz said.

"Or being tortured in prison," said Melake. "Your brother died fast, you said. From a single bullet."

I thought of Joas and the ledge under which he lay, covered by rocks. Somehow I could not cry, but only remembered that same moment over and over, him standing to see all around and the shot ringing so, then the echo. I would hear that sound in my dreams forever. Forever I would see that small round hole in his back, and the circle of blood around it. So small a thing stands between life and death, a tiny round hole.

As we walked, the landscape flattened. And now on the road we saw other travelers, some with bundles and furniture and children or old people on their backs, walking, walking, perhaps to feeding stations like the Muslims we had met the night before. It was an exodus.

I glanced at Almaz. Her eyes were still badly swollen, two lumps under them, and her head cut from that rock those evil children threw. I noticed again how thin she was, her skinny legs showing, for the bottom of her dress was ripped, her feet bare.

"When we come to water," I said, "Almaz must bathe her face."

"What happened to her?"

"A long journey," I said grimly.

"She is good for a child. She does not complain."

"No use to complain," I said. "We are going to Jerusalem."

But even the thought of Jerusalem left me empty, for Joas was not with us.

Dan and Weizero Channa met us like *zamed*, with blessings and joy, and Weizero kissing me, plenty. Her face folded into its deep lines when she heard about Joas, and she trembled. "Poor girl, brave girl, how you did have to suffer!"

I thought of Kess Haim, so powerful, now imprisoned, and I said, "I grieve for Kess Haim."

"My heart aches for him," said Weizero Channa. "But what can we do?"

"Without enough money to buy their way out . . ."
Dan lifted his hands, dropped them helplessly to his sides.

His eyes were bloodshot from weariness and worry. "My father would not carry a rifle. He hated shooting."

"It would not have helped him," said his grandmother. "Dan, your father will endure this. At least we know he is alive."

Her expression went to dreaming; she was tired and laid her head back.

Dan looked more sober than ever, worried, pulling, pulling at his lower lip. He was glad to see us in the first moment, yes, but soon his expression changed. We were a burden, that was plain to see.

Dan frowned deeply, pulling at his lip as he asked, "What did you do with Joas?"

I was startled. Quickly I lowered my eyes. "I buried him."

"How?"

"What? I—we made a hole. We covered him with leaves, then with rocks." I was shocked at his questions, and now a strange anger took hold of me, and a hate. Dan, standing there frowning, pulling at his lower lip and so stern, Dan was alive while my brother Joas was dead.

Dan persisted. "Did you wrap him? Did you wash him?"

"Dan, there was no water near, nothing . . ."

"Did you offer prayers?"

I looked at Dan, then at Melake. "What did you expect I would do?" I cried. "Call a priest? Find ten mourners? I did what I could!" Tears pushed against my chest, but I refused to release them, for my anger overpowered grief.

"Desta, I am only asking because . . ."

"How can you ask me these things?" I cried out. "You

were sitting here, resting on thick leaves. My brother was dead, and we were alone. I had no prayers to give, no shroud, no water, no help!"

Dan turned, his head down, hands folded inside his *shamma*. "I am sorry," he said, his head lifted, eyes to a distance, avoiding my face. "I only asked because if you had not been able to bury Joas, we would go back and do it."

Melake cleared his throat and scraped his foot around in the dust.

"I see. Well, everything has been done," I said, turning away to hide my shame. "When do we leave?" I said harshly. "We are ready."

"We'll go when Kasa returns," said Dan. "We must decide which way."

"What do you mean?"

"Kasa says it is at least ten days more to the border. Maybe longer. Walking at night, it is slow. And with the litter to carry . . . we can still turn back and return to our villages. We were talking before you came. Trying to decide. Now you are here, and without my father and Joas . . ." Dan paused, stammering. Did he mean it was improper for us to travel together? That Weizero wasn't chaperone enough? Or did he mean he no longer wanted me. Oh, after all the days of sorrow, this anger felt fine and strong. It pounded in my cheeks, pushed against my chest—beautiful rage!

"We want to go to Jerusalem," I said, stern, hard.

"The guide will want payment," Dan said. "Do you have money?"

"Don't worry," I said sharply. "I have everything we

need, even money. My aunt did not send me poor," I added.

Dan sighed.

"I have money," I repeated.

"I would have given you some," Dan said softly.

"Thank you, then," I said grudgingly.

"For no reason," he said politely, but still he did not look at me, only to the distance.

I went to Weizero Channa. She sat leaning against a tree trunk, exhausted.

I said, "Weizero Channa, you are the eldest among us. What do you wish to do?"

Weizero opened her mouth, exposing few teeth there, and dark. "It is not for me to have wishes," she said, "for I am being carried, not walking much. It is for the young people to say."

Scabs had formed around her lips, from insect bites, and she shook with weariness, while the bones of her fingers were knotted and swollen. She must be in great pain, I thought, and I said, "But can you endure this journey, Weizero Channa? Ten or twelve days more, and then to wait longer still in Sudan?"

She nodded. "It is only my body," she said.

"What about Kess Haim and the others? Is it right for us to leave them here in prison, to go to Jerusalem without them?" Never before have I questioned my elders; these were strange times.

There was a silent space. Then Weizero spoke. "In my dream when the ram came to deliver the lambs, still the lambs had to follow. They did not waver. Each one had to lift himself up and do this thing alone."

The answer settled over us. Dan said, "When we began this journey, my father and I made a vow. We said if something should happen to one of us, the other would take Weizero Channa to Jerusalem, as long as she wanted to go."

"Of course I want to go!" cried Weizero, her voice suddenly shrill. "This is the hour of our redemption! I will not be left behind."

"We would never leave you, Grandmother," said Dan, the leader now.

A moment later someone broke into our little glade, announcing, "*Sille!* All's well, Kasa has found you."

The guide wore a loose white tunic, a white cloth round his head, and a trader's bag slung over his shoulder. On his back he carried a water jug, on his head a basket filled with various foods, and on top of these a bundle of leaves tied with hemp—*qat*.

He was round-faced and leathery from wind and sun, his teeth stained from *qat*, and now he was on the way up to joy. I could see it in his eyes, the gleeful way he rubbed his hands together and the wetness of his mouth.

"So! Which way will it be? It matters little to me. My life is moving, walking, guiding, so it matters not, west or east, only you must decide."

"We are going to Sudan," said Dan, turning from me, speaking to the guide. "Did you bring us food?"

"Yes, yes, of course," said Kasa. "What do you take me for, a thief? I brought you grain, as much as possible for the few coins you gave me."

He swung down a small sack, gave it to Dan, who looked at it in disbelief. "Kasa," he said, "I gave you twenty *burr*. What else did you bring us?"

140

"Ah. Some lovely turnips. Onions. Plenty, plenty." Two small bundles came from his pack, and Dan took them, shaking his head.

"No eggs?"

"The eggs in that market were not worth buying," said Kasa with a smile. He picked a leaf from his bundle, held it to his nose, savoring the smell before he rolled it up carefully and put it into his mouth, between the cheek and gum, to relish its juices. He looked at me now. "You want a guide?"

"Yes."

"And the child, too?"

"Yes, of course."

"You have money?"

"A little."

"The trip is one hundred *burr*," he said with a broad smile.

I looked at Dan. Deliberately he turned away, toward the stream.

Melake made himself busy folding up blankets.

Weizero Channa hobbled to the sack of vegetables, picked them out, smelling the turnips and the onions one by one.

I faced the guide, my eyes straight ahead, not meeting his, but not downcast, either. "Did every person pay you one hundred *burr*?" I asked.

"Of course they did. Every one. Even the children. That is the cost. After all, I take a risk. I have just spent two days in prison, and I tell you, it was not pleasant for me there."

"If they paid you one hundred *burr* to go all the way,"

I said, "then I must pay you only half. We are closer now," I added. "Much."

Kasa's mouth fell open. He stared at me, glowering, then suddenly he began to laugh. "A girl with schooling! Ha ha! So, you tell me what is right for money? Very well. Very well. So, how much do you pay me to take you?"

"Fifty *burr*," I said firmly.

"But there are two of you!" he cried, shrieking with laughter now as the *qat* took hold. "Two of you, so it is one hundred *burr* just the same, ha ha ha!"

"I do not have one hundred *burr*," I said, my voice very soft, eyes downcast.

Kasa shook his head. "No money, no guide."

"I will give you fifty," I said. "My sister will not take any extra time for you."

"I have a price," said the guide. "You want me to starve? I have children. Family. I have expenses, plenty."

"I have only fifty *burr*," I said. "No more."

It went on and on, round and round. By turns, Kasa laughed, got a dark look on his face, shook his fist, scraped his feet. By now the others stood waiting, ready. They would say nothing; a person's barter is his own business, always. On and on, round and round. At last Kasa said, "You have jewels?"

"No."

"A young woman like you?" cried Kasa, angry now and feeling he must bluster in front of the others. I felt equally so; I was not going to be cut down by this man.

"Fifty *burr* is a fair price," I said. "I will fetch your water for you," I added, knowing I had to offer something more to save his pride.

"You have beads, I am sure," Kasa said. "You have possessions. A knife? A rifle? Ha ha. Give me beads, then, and we will say no more. It is getting dark."

"I gave you a fair offer," I said. "I will draw your water; you have no woman here to do it."

Somehow that angered him. I don't know why; maybe he was just coming down from the *qat*.

"Can we stand here all night arguing?" he cried. "Everyone will be in danger because of you. Look, I will leave you here; you may be eaten by hyenas, what do I care? Is it my worry? I do what I can. I try to be a friend to every traveler, to help them, even to go against the Dergue at the risk of my neck, and then I must stand here and be insulted by a woman, late into the night with my stomach rumbling from hunger—no, it is not enough."

I turned from him, took the cloth from my pack, and wordlessly I handed him the coins and one of the golden bracelets.

He took it, bit down on it, hard. Then he said coldly, "You must give me the other one also."

"I have no other."

"You lie. These bracelets are always in a pair."

"I have no other." I looked straight into his eyes. "I swear it."

Satisfied, Kasa took the golden hoop and put it into his bag.

My two golden hoop bracelets were safe in my bundle, but the lie burned in my mouth.

I sighed as I took up my things and we set out.

12

THE FIRST PART OF THE JOURNEY WAS EASY COMPARED TO the second. Before, we had moved on familiar ground. The blue-green hills always beckoned, friendly, like arms we have known since birth. Now the landscape was different, with unfamiliar trees, then vast spaces with no trees at all, then patches of thick jungle with flies and insects ready to suck our blood.

Almaz suffered from the insects; her blood must be sweet indeed. Dan saw her swatting, and he took pity. He made her a flyswatter from a stick and a bunch of cattails tied to it with reeds. Our elders usually carry swatters made of horse-hair, but the cattail swatter was a pleasure to Almaz, and she thanked Dan with a look of pure joy and carried the swatter always.

I had no extra clothes. My holiday *shamma* lay buried with Joas, and my extra skirt I had given to Almaz, for hers was torn beyond wearing. I had to make a hole in the waist and tie it around her; still, it hung.

As we walked I followed Dan and Melake who followed the guide, carrying Weizero Channa, and sometimes they talked to each other or to Almaz, sometimes to me. For the first time in my life, words stayed locked tight inside of me. What good were words? Now and then a single word leaped to the surface, like the bubble in a jug of water. "Joas!" But quickly it was drowned again in the water, and the thought lay at the bottom of a thick, sluggish pool, like the pools we encountered where the water was putrid.

I slept badly, as if my eyes were wide open and I were ready to spring, defending Almaz. With each awakening I heard that single sound again, the shot that had killed Joas.

Then I raised myself up and set out vigorously walking, walking, my whole mind set on pushing through the undergrowth, stepping down just so, making myself numb to the pain in my foot that was hot and festering, wiping off the sweat, walking, walking, until my mind clouded over again.

"I am praying every day and night for your brother," Dan told me, as he prepared for his morning prayers on the third day. He glanced at me strangely. He was changing, too.

"Thank you."

I watched Dan swaying, his eyes closed as if he were in his own synagogue. I could hear the sounds of the wilderness and the laughter of Kasa who gossiped with a companion. But Dan seemed deaf to all of it, lost in God. I have never been so good at praying, shutting out the world. And since that dawn at the grave I found no prayers in me at all.

When Dan was finished he came and sat down by me. Nearby Melake was trying to mend a torn sandal; Weizero

Channa nodded and dozed, with Almaz beside her. "I grieve for your brother," Dan said. He was serious, frowning, yet settled down, as for a conversation.

I shook my head, resisting.

"He was a good friend," Dan persisted. "And he knew how to laugh." Dan laughed slightly himself.

I sighed, turning my face away.

"I remember how white his teeth shone when he laughed—a fine face. Everyone said how handsome he was, that Joas."

Unwillingly I answered, high-pitched, "Yes."

"He used to play pranks in our village, plenty. Once he caught a small green snake—harmless, but wriggling, and put it into the hole where our weaver sits—ugh! How that man did leap with fright, and the strings attached to his toes were jiggling so!" Dan smiled at the memory, his face glistening.

I felt too strange, as if a curtain around me were tearing, tearing, and something terrible leaking in, too sweet, too sad.

Dan went on, nodding, and slightly swaying, not looking at me but to the distance, letting memories take him. "Oh, he always made us laugh—yes, he was good at laughing and making a joke. That is the thing I remember about Joas. And the elders in our village all said how he was good with words. The most difficult passages, Joas learned them."

I cleared my throat, and something cleared in my mind, remembering. "He never was without that Hebrew primer in his pocket," I whispered.

"Well, but he knew it! That was the fine thing about

Joas, you see. It is not often we find a man who can laugh so well but still be smart, plenty smart, yes. And brave. Your brother was always the one to start on a venture, always first to set out."

I breathed deep, saying, "Even if he did not know the way."

"He sought ways. He looked for trails. Always. Wasn't he the first to say it? That we could go to Zion? I remember, when I first told the dream, how he looked, that fire in his eyes . . . do you remember?"

Words. Never, never had Dan said so many words to me. Suddenly he seemed a different person.

"I remember everything about Joas," Dan went on. "I think of him all the time. Don't you think of him? All the things you did? How he was such a good brother to you and to Almaz? He always talked about you, how he would bring you to Zion."

Something tore loose in me and spoke out. "Yes! Oh, yes I remember. He talked and worked, he saved his money, hiding it in a hole. He said we were meant to go to Jerusalem, and I didn't listen at first, but only fought with him. Joas could see the truth. Joas knew so much better than I that our lives were wrong, but I was afraid, where he was brave. My brother was so brave!"

It was less like talk than like praying, saying words not to tell each other something new, but because we needed to say his name, to affirm that Joas lived and we loved him, yes! And now he was dead.

I told Dan how Joas led Almaz and me, always stepping out so boldly, hardly sleeping, protecting us. "Joas went ahead to find the way, gave us his food if there wasn't enough, cautioned us about the water."

On and on now the memories poured out, "Joas even broke the commandments for us, so that we could live. But he tried to be good, Dan! He told us to keep Shabbat in our hearts, to say the prayers in our minds as we walked."

"May his memory be blessed," said Dan. He sounded like his father, Kess Haim. A comfort.

"The day the *shifta* caught him, he was looking for you, but making sure Almaz and I would be safe. Everything I know, Joas taught me. Everything. Every dream I have, Joas gave to me!"

"So," said Dan, exhaling hard, looking at me now deeply, "your brother still lives in you. And in Almaz. How lucky you are, Desta, to live with his memory inside you!"

In the next moment Dan was gone, and I sat quite alone, but yet not alone, surrounded by feelings of such pain and such sweetness mingled together that I was no longer aware of time or place or being, only of this feeling deep in me, spreading to every fiber of me. Joas is dead. Joas, my brother, beloved brother. Oh, God!

I wept.

Later, much later, I awakened to see Weizero Channa bending over me.

"Come, Desta, let me see your foot," she said.

"My foot is fine."

"Let me see!"

Her old eyes, while watery, were sharp. She had seen how I turned my body from the pain, for the old wound had never healed, but grew wider and softer each day with a yellow pool of pus in the center.

Weizero sat down on the ground, made me put my foot in her lap, and she shook her head, sighing, clucking so. "Uh, uh, this is not good. How did this come to you? Oh, you must take care of this, Desta."

"I put my foot down wrongly," I said. "Thorns."

"The foot is inflamed! Dan, bring the herbs from my pack. Quick, now!"

Weizero Channa made me a poultice and laid it onto my poor foot, and oh, I could feel the healing seeping into it, and with it she murmured words, maybe prayers, maybe incantations, and she sat stroking my leg, rubbing and kneading the muscles, rolling out the pain, and as she did so, again the tears flowed from me, a river of tears, on and on and on, and old Weizero Channa—how I love her for it!—only went on murmuring, pretending not to notice.

Water lay warm and sluggish in a pool by the road. Green ooze covered the surface. We dipped our jars in deep, but still we brought up slime, and we had to drink it. One thing we knew: Without water death comes quickly. So we traded. We slipped away from death only to welcome disease.

We all got sick from the water. Cramps. Diarrhea. Fever. All except for Kasa, who strode ahead, his arms swinging, and sometimes he even let loose a sudden shriek of joy. Kasa, born to this climate, stayed robust.

As we broke through the jungle growth, we saw occasional wanderers, refugees, moving like ghosts, none talking, for they, like we, needed every breath just to keep moving. Were they Jews? Were they Christians or Muslims or even pagans? It did not matter anymore; they were so wretched, with their eyes sunken and their faces set, and I thought, how horrible. They had traveled much longer than we, coming from Eritrea and Tigre, as we learned from hearing snatches of talk. Their faces haunted me, with large eyes, somehow looking too very old, and yet like children.

We had been out about three weeks, and I was still strong enough, but poor Almaz, weak from the start, suffered plenty. Melake, too, took it badly in his body. Weight fell from him; we could see it in his face and his ribs. He held down no food, and with his misery he became more and more like a child, settling into the orders given by Kasa or by Dan. And Dan tended him. "Time to rest, Melake! Get off your feet, old friend, there, and put down your pack."

Weizero Channa made a good beginning every night. She walked, holding Dan's arm. Soon she was upon the litter, held on Dan's shoulder and Melake's. The two boys carried her as if she had no weight, and it is true, her bones were like sticks. But her eyes were bright, and every morning and evening she called out, "Joy! It is sunrise." (Or sunset). "You see, the heavens are over us, no matter where, and God is watching!"

One day Almaz found a body at the side of the road. "Desta!" she cried, pointing.

I rushed to see. I shuddered. "Don't look," I told her.

We walked by night and on into early morning, stopping to rest. As we went, the air became heavy with heat, heavier each day; what little water we found became warm, then hot in our jugs.

Some days it was all I could do to bring down one foot after the other, with no strength for thoughts, shallow or deep. Yet other days sent me into a trance so pure that I

150

forgot my body completely, my mind fastening upon a thought, then another, probing and twisting the way my fingers used to pick at the knots in a ball of twine. Then, hunger and thirst were forgotten; I caught a glimpse of what it must be like for holy men who live in meditation.

Sometimes in my mind Dan became Joas, and I almost called him by the wrong name. I thought of him like a brother, or as my friend, never anymore as my betrothed, and I wondered, should it be so between wife and husband? Shame was gone between us, and strangeness, and I wondered, should it be so?

He spoke to Almaz more than to me, but always I had the feeling he was saying words through her for my ears. "It won't be long now," he said one morning as we came to rest. "You are a good traveler, little one."

"I did not travel well today," she admitted in a soft voice. "Desta carried me."

"What?" Dan turned. "Is this true?"

I shrugged. "Only a little way."

"You will exhaust yourself. Melake and I will go by turns, one carrying Weizero, the other can take Almaz. She is like a fly. I can easily carry Almaz on my back." Dan stood up, lifting Almaz to show me his strength.

"No," I said. "Almaz is my sister."

For an instant I thought he would be stormy and remind me, we are betrothed! Almaz is going to be my relative, too! But he said only, "It isn't good for Almaz if you become ill. Please don't be stubborn. Let us help you."

The land turned bleak and treeless. Desert. Oh, how vast and how desolate . . . as far as the eye can see the sky

151

makes a rim touching the land; the sky turns white with the heat, and nothing grows except for a few trees twisted by the sudden ferocity of desert storms. Here, water is too abundant or too scarce, never right for holding life. It is a strange and terrifying place, the desert, especially for us, who come from the green-blue mountains in the highlands.

Kasa rubbed his hands when he told us we would soon be at the border. "Tomorrow! Tomorrow!" he said eagerly. "Then we part. A bargain is a bargain—at the border I leave you."

We stopped after the night's journey, making our beds as usual, from a blanket or skin drawn over into a clump of thorny bushes, sparse shelter, for true.

Dan came to me. It reminded me of Joas, how he used to scratch two twigs together outside our *tukel*.

"What will we do at the border, Dan?" I whispered so as not to wake the others, and Dan sat beside me, his *shamma* drawn up to his face not for warmth, but for modesty. I smiled to myself. How strange for the two of us to be sitting here, talking alone.

"There will be soldiers, I think, with guns," Dan said. "We must be very careful. Very quiet. Kasa said he will bring us to a place where it is not so hard to cross, only a shallow ravine."

"We will walk across? Is that all?"

"It won't be easy," Dan said. "We'll wait until dark, then run across, very fast, very silently. I'll carry Weizero. Melake can carry Almaz."

"I want to take Almaz across, Dan," I said. "Really. It is something I must do." I had a strong feeling for this, and my heart pounded. "For my family," I added.

152

Dan sighed. "Yes. I understand." He added, "But you must be very careful. We will watch and then run. Maybe we cannot all go at the same time. When you start, you must hurry and not look back. Do you understand?"

"Of course," I said. "I will do it."

"Once we are across," Dan said, "we must find the camp."

"The camp?" Strange, I had not thought of what we would do after crossing the border. Now I wondered what lay ahead. "What is in the camp?"

"Well, I think it is a place to rest," Dan said. "That's all I know. My father said we would go to a camp and wait there to be called."

"Called? How, Dan? By whom?"

He shrugged. "We will be called. That's all I know. Desta, if we should become separated . . ."

"How could we? We're all together, we go together!"

"I mean if for some reason . . . Desta," he said solemnly, frowning, "if anything should happen to me, would you take care of Weizero?"

"Of course. Melake would, too. And you would take care of Almaz in case I . . ."

"Yes. Of course."

We stood up. Dan's eyes did not leave my face. He said, "We can shake hands, Desta. It is a bargain, isn't it?"

"Yes," I said softly. Our hands touched and clasped and held. In that moment I had strange feelings, not at all the same feelings I ever had from touching my brother.

* * *

It was late afternoon. Kasa drew us aside, pointing. Beyond we saw only desolation, the gray-brown sand, now and then a twisted row of trees, their flat little leaves bleached out to a gray color, their roots knotted and jagged from the harshness of this land.

"The border," Kasa said. "Walk. You will see."

"Shouldn't we wait until dark?"

"Ah, don't worry so. The guards sleep in the hut, chewing *qat,* drinking *tedge;* they hear nothing, see nothing!"

"Then why don't you come with us?" Dan asked.

The guide's face changed, his eyes thundering suddenly, and he railed, "What is it with you people? Never satisfied? I risk my life, I bring you here where we agreed, and now you want me to go with you into Sudan?"

"No, no, just to the place . . ."

"There is no place, don't you see? You go there, there, by the side of the hut, across that hill, and you will see it. Bushes to hide you. You lie there until dark. Go! Go!"

"Kasa, maybe you could keep the guards busy, engage them in talk, while we slip across."

"What? What? You want Kasa to tell lies? To get trouble, plenty, maybe prison again? Go! Go!"

He turned, brushing off Dan's hand as he would swat away an insect, and we saw his robe fluttering behind him, and then we were alone.

We walked. We saw straight before us then the sagging hut, the colorless clump of thorny bushes, an inhospitable barrier, and beyond, the ravine, dipping down, sloping upward on the other side, laced with barbed wire.

Cruel hooks hung down from the wire, to catch the flesh. We all gazed at those hooks, speechless.

Dan sighed deeply. "Come."

Behind the thorny bushes we lay nearly flat, waiting for darkness. Meanwhile I saw Dan searching with his eyes, and at last he pointed, whispering, "There—the wire is raised there and broken. Keep the place in your mind. See? Make a line to it in your mind, and when I tell you, then run. Run. And don't look back. Do you hear?"

"Yes! Yes!" I breathed, my heart hammering, making ready to leap. I whispered to Almaz. "Be ready to run." She did not want to be carried; I could feel her muscles tensed and ready.

Still we waited, and as darkness fell I became aware of other bodies, people creeping up behind us, breathing, waiting. Turning, I saw a pair of eyes shining white, then someone darted out. Footsteps crunched and scraped. I held my breath. Across. He was across! I plucked at Dan's arm. "Now?"

"Wait."

Others began to stir. Shapes, dark and formless, noise, grunting. Another one across. Another one. It was like the children's game of *debebkosh,* a dangerous hide and seek. We heard the rumblings of voices from within the hut, an occasional burst of laughter, then a shout, the voices toned between pleasure and cruelty: Soldiers with time hanging heavy upon them, too idle, feel the burden of lonesome duty and are quick to laugh—or to shoot.

Dan raised his finger. A signal.

But something happened.

The door of the hut opened. The guards came out, laughing, slamming the door back against the hut and grunting loud like dogs looking for prey. We heard the clinking of their rifles, and they slung them around in readiness.

"Patrol!" Dan breathed. "They're going on patrol, oh, God, God!"

Suddenly lights flashed on, wide beams of light from a truck cutting paths into the sand, moving closer, closer.

My eyes fastened on the lights, and my heart leaped while the flesh on my back crawled together. Closer the light came, and with it the heat, the smell of danger.

"Run!" Dan screamed, loud like a rifle shot, and in that same moment he hurled himself toward the light, toward the guards with their rifles, heading them off.

We ran. I pulled Almaz, running, running with no other thought but the thunder of motion and fear and panic all hurling together. Run! Run! My blood shouted it into my ears. Run! Run! My feet pounded into the ground, slipped and scraped. I rolled down into the ravine, still grasping Almaz tight, so tight that she rolled down after, then I rose, pulled her harder under the wire, my lungs bursting with the need to stop, my mind commanding me to go. Go! I heard something tear. I heard Almaz cry out. Still I surged, my mind fast on Dan's warning: Don't look back.

We ran until I had no more breath and my throat was on fire. I realized then that we had left behind our water jug. It was a terrible loss.

Almaz and I lay there, panting and spent. Moments later Melake came to us carrying Weizero Channa.

At the sight of them I cried out in spite of myself. "Melake! Weizero! Oh, thank God."

"Dan! Where is Dan?" cried Almaz, not understanding what Dan had done for us.

"My grandson saved us," sobbed Weizero Channa. "He

held off the guards. They would have captured us all. Oh, God! God! It is not right that the young must sacrifice for the old—they should have taken me!"

We could not look into each other's eyes, for we were ashamed of being the survivors. Painfully I asked myself, would I have done as much for him? How would I ever make my life worthy of having been saved? Dan! Joas! Who am I, that first brother and then friend gives himself for me? Sobs rose in my chest, but there was no time to let them go.

Weizero moaned, swaying. Her cheeks blew in and out with every breath.

"We must keep moving," I said sharply. "Melake! We have to keep moving. Get up, Melake. Can you carry Weizero? Yes, you are strong enough. Come, we have to find the camp." I became aware of motion. Other people. A trail cut into the land. "There is a road. We'll move with the others. *Come.*"

The dawn's light laid yellow fingers over the land, and it was desolate indeed, sand and sand as far as the eye could see, ripples in the sand to trick us into believing that life lay beyond, when really it was only more desolation and sometimes the bones of a beast, camel, or goat, and maybe some bones of man, too.

As I looked out over this hopeless dawn, I closed my eyes against this sight and against the horrors that I knew awaited Dan. The guards would beat him. They would question him. They would take him to prison and keep him there. How long?

I looked at Weizero, her legs bowed and trembling, at Almaz with her puckering mouth and deep-set eyes, at Melake, who shifted his eyes helplessly, his face seeming flat, with all the light gone out of it.

Already I felt the weight of the heat, though it was only daybreak.

"We have to walk," I said, "before the heat comes."

"Where?" said Melake.

"That way. West." I had always been the follower before. Now I was the leader. I looked from one to the other of these three. For a moment I felt only that terrible weight and the thought that I might lie down here and die. I said to Melake, "Do you have money?"

"Dan had the money," said Melake.

"Maybe it will help him," I said grimly.

"Even with money," said Melake, "there is nothing here to buy."

"Someone will pass by here," I said, feeling a surge of impatience, and needing it. "I still have my gold bracelets," I said. "We'll trade for food."

"And if nobody comes?" Almaz whispered.

"Something will come to us," I said harshly, and I knew my eyes were angry, as Joas's had been at the beginning when I doubted him. "Come now! We have to keep moving while we still have some strength. Almaz, are you strong enough to walk?"

"Yes."

I saw her sway, knew the lie, but nodded. "Good."

We walked. Soon the sun was a shimmering, blazing ball. Around my lips and over my brows the skin blistered. A fine sand blew into our mouths and eyes; we covered our faces with our rags; still the sun blazed down upon us and beyond, spread shimmering streaks across the land. We looked down at our feet, and we wasted nothing, not the blink of an eye or the flick of a hand. Flies settled upon us. It was nothing, only one more small burden laid upon a body that was already spent. Step. Step. One more step. I thought only of this, nothing of home or heart, not even of Almaz, only this: Step.

They followed me, Melake with Weizero on his back, Almaz dragging behind. I heard the faint plodding of their feet, but I did not turn. My senses filled with their steps; the world had been narrowed to this: feet touching sand in a rhythm that must not break.

We walked until spots jumped before our eyes. "Rest," I said. Melake and I spread his *shamma* between some thistles, raising a patch of shade. We huddled there. My tongue felt thick in my mouth. Melake's eyes burned with fever. Almaz and Weizero Channa lay on the sand, each small thin body a curve, a wisp, with breath coming shallow and swift.

Other people passed, walking skeletons. An old man dropped at the roadside. I watched. He no longer moved. I knew he was dead. I told Melake, "Get his water jug."

Melake only stared at me.

I pulled myself up, and with sudden fury I hurried to the fallen man's side, my eyes darting about for others who might swoop down upon my prize.

Swiftly I snatched up the jug and ran with it to my people.

We finished all the water in the jug; if we left the last bit, the heat would only consume it.

Three days we walked in that fiery furnace, each day seeing more and more others, miserable and silent as shadows.

But what did I know of misery then? I had not yet seen the refugee camp in Sudan.

13

AT FIRST THERE WAS ONLY THE SOUND, LIKE A DISTANT BUZZ-
ing and humming of a thousand bees. Then the smell came
to us in great nauseating waves; smells of human decay. I
had never smelled it before, but I knew what it was. So did
the others. Still we went ahead.

"Is it the camp?" Almaz whispered between cracked
lips.

"Yes, it is," I said.

"Praise God!" called out Weizero Channa, then lay back
against Melake, her eyes closed to the sights that now un-
folded.

At first we saw nothing except the mass of bodies, dark-
skinned, many naked altogether, a jungle of bones, bare arms
and legs, a forest of round skulls, the skin stretched tight,
the eyes shining as they do when only a sparse ray of life
remains. They sat with ripples of movement falling over them,
moving and fluttering all in a body, but only slightly, so weak
they could think of nothing but taking in air, waiting for

the next breath. Yet they sat with great dignity, quiet, accepting fate, waiting.

Famine. It was too harsh. It was an indecency to the eye, to the soul. Famine had touched them all. Later I learned there were ten thousand of them here, and thousands upon thousands more in other camps. Who can imagine such numbers?

I looked. I heaved. With no food inside me, I brought up only sour stuff and shook all over from it.

"My God," breathed Melake. "Desta, is this the place?"

"It has to be," I whispered back. "We can't go any further."

Melake set Weizero Channa down. "Are we in Jerusalem?" she breathed.

"Not yet, Weizero, not yet," Melake said tenderly, wiping her brow with his *shamma*.

He and I stood together, squinting against the glare. In the distance we could make out huts of straw, some patched with tin, tents, shelters constructed of boxes and boards. It was huge, larger than any village I had ever seen, a town set into the middle of the desert with everything gray and over all that wailing sound of wind and human voices together.

We looked again, saw a building of strange white stone, square and official. Over the door hung a sign.

"Can you read it?" I asked Melake.

"No," he said. "But with writing over the door, it must be the place to go."

A line of people stood outside waiting, and as we drew near I thought of the line of our people coming down the mountain from Segid, proud and purified, some with horns, others with Torah, the women with babies on their backs. Now, too, I saw such women, but the babies lay with their heads back and mouths open, like young birds begging for food but no longer able to cry. I saw three small boys, naked, sitting on a rock, their heads down and picking at their fingers with sharp sticks. The fingers were red stumps from picking and prodding, the boys trying to get out the parasites that creep under the skin, for the itching makes one crazy. I saw a man, with only a rag loosely tied around his loins, holding a dead boy in his arms, looking for a place to set him down. He found no place, but circled and circled, his face without expression, and nobody to notice.

I reached for Melake's hand. He pressed my fingers, tight.

I took Almaz close beside me, and we went into the line of people. Weizero Channa slumped cross-legged, her head bent down, as if she sat quite at peace under her own tree outside her own *tukel*. I glanced at her, then at Melake. He shook his head.

A boy about the same age as Almaz suddenly rushed up, smiling and chattering, bobbing and looking miraculously happy. More than the sight of the ravaged others, this jolted me. I gasped.

"Hallo!" he cried, pointing to himself, "I am Hagos, and you are new, am I right?"

Almaz reached toward him, dazed.

"You hear my words? You speak my language? Oh, please."

"We understand," I murmured, smiling in spite of myself, for the boy leaped up into the air, and now his chatter did not stop.

162

"Ah, that is so good. Many people here are Arabs, you know, and I speak no Arabic, just a few words. Those from Eritrea and Tigre speak only their tongues. I am from the border, you see, and so I look for people who can talk Amharic to me. What are your names? When did you arrive? Yes, you must stand in this line. Here they will greet you, give you the needle if you are dying. Are any of you dying? Ah, maybe the old one, but she will get the magic needle, you will see. Sometimes the needle comes too late. We have old ones dying all the time, young ones too, you will see. I will take you to a hut, and you can see people dying there, but first you must stand here to get your portion."

For Almaz, the sight of this boy just her size had a strange effect. She seemed to come alive, and now she and he talked while Melake and I looked on, our hands still touching.

"Why are you here, Hagos?" Almaz chirped. "Who are you? Are you sent to welcome us?"

The boy laughed. "I am always here," he said. "I have always *been* here. I can remember nothing else."

"What about your parents?"

He shrugged.

"Who takes care of you?"

"The white ones!" Hagos exclaimed. "You will see. They give me water and grain and oil."

"Where do you sleep?"

"There." Hagos pointed to the tangle of bodies all sitting on mats in the blazing sun, waiting.

"Have you no *tukel*?" asked Almaz.

The boy's face became furrowed. "I—I used to have a hut," he said. "I think I once had a hut. I cannot remember. It does not matter. Sometimes at sunset the water truck comes.

And sometimes there is a truck with food. Unless it breaks on the way. You have to look out for the *shifta*," he said. "I will tell you when they come to the camp. Then you must hide your possessions. Do you have money? Possessions?"

"No," I said hastily. "We have only our rags here, that are on our backs."

"Sometimes they are angry when people have nothing, and they beat them. Except," he said with a smile, "they never catch me."

By now the smell seemed to be less. I wondered at it. Then I knew: We were getting used to it. Now, too, I saw shades of differences; some people were moving, collecting scraps of dung or twigs to make small fires. A haze hung over a portion of the camp. Far in the distance a truck stood, with a man guarding it proudly, while several other men bent to look into the engine.

"Who are they, Hagos?" I pointed.

"Officials," he said. "They give us food."

"Who sends them?"

Hagos shrugged. "God?"

As we stood the line behind us grew. People came from every direction. A few rode camels. Some sat on donkeys. Most walked. All the weeks we remained in the camp, more people came every day.

"Where do they come from?" Almaz asked.

Hagos lifted his hands, smiling broadly. "Everywhere."

"But why?"

"To live here!" Hagos exclaimed.

"Here?"

Groups of children circled round and round together. I

saw one little boy pick up a stick and hit a little girl with it on the legs. She huddled down.

I saw a white man wearing a red shirt and blue jeans leaning on a shovel. He was digging a deep hole. The grave digger, I thought, but Hagos turned to me and pointed. "He is from America. His name is Douglas. He is digging for water."

I stared at the man. His hair was a bushy mass of yellow curls. The blue kerchief tied around his neck reminded me of the blue headcloth I once owned.

We approached the hut with the sign, and I saw the uneven letters UNESCO and wished I could read. Empty boxes stood outside the strange building, with letters also—Save the Children. Catholic Relief. Product of West Germany. Canada. USA.

Now and then a person darted up, took an empty box, disappeared with it. Two women fought over a box, tearing it to pieces.

Outside the hut a cloth canopy had been stretched where two white men stood, and from inside came a woman, back and forth, the three of them sweating and coughing, plenty, and their shirts stained with sweat.

They spoke in words we could not understand. Their teeth were so fine! Large and firm, none rotten or broken. The woman had very fine yellow hair and pale skin. She wore pants like a man and sandals. Her hands were covered with small cuts and she coughed heavily, but she did not stop her motions, swift and gentle, or her talking, which was soothing to my ears.

She looked into my eyes, felt my head, took Almaz's

wrists to feel for something there. Ah, these white ones are so beautiful, I thought, looking down, ashamed of my rags, of the way my stomach rumbled, of the pain that came suddenly like a knife in my middle. Somebody pointed to the fields, and I ran to relieve myself, with Almaz clinging to my arm, for she would not leave me.

When I returned the white ones had Weizero Channa down on a low litter made of strings. It was as Hagos said. They had a needle. They spoke as they worked, though I understood nothing, only the sounds, so strange.

"What are they saying?" I asked Hagos. "Can you speak their language?"

"They speak English," said Hagos. "I can understand a little, but not speak the words. They say the water truck is broken down again. They say they want to give your old one the water needle."

"What is that?"

"A water bag on a needle, put into the arm, to keep them alive. But they don't have enough of the bags. They say all the needles are gone, with so many people having cholera."

More talk, sharp, rushing back and forth between the white ones, and they were wiping their faces, scowling, angry.

"Why are they angry?" I asked Hagos.

"Oh, because the people keep dying. And they do not know what to do with the corpses. Sometimes nobody claims the body, and they must get it out in the pile to make room for more sick, like this old one here."

The white man looked at Almaz, into her eyes, shaking his head and his lips tight. He motioned to her stomach, to mine, to his own.

"He wants to know whether you have the cramps."

"Yes."

The medicine man gave me white pills, then a small cup with water. It was beautiful, delicate, and small, of white paper. I drank, swallowing the pill, then gave it to Almaz. Carefully I handed back the small cup. He shook his head, smiling.

Hagos laughed. "You can keep it."

The cup was mine, this small paper thing, so beautiful. I cradled it in my hand.

Now another man came over, a black man wearing a white headcloth and jodhpurs and a ragged shirt. The black man spoke to us.

"What are you?" he said harshly. "Where are you from?"

"Ethiopia," I said.

"Are you Falashas?"

"We are Ethiopians," said Melake.

"Very well. This is how it is: You will get grain when the truck comes. Oil, also. You can bake your own *injera*. If you are able to work, sometimes there is work in fields nearby, no wages. Food only. A truck comes before daylight. If you want to work," he motioned with his hand, "be there. They look you over and pick out the strong ones. The farmers do not like it when their workers die in the fields."

No water truck came that night. We laid ourselves down, grateful for the darkness, and that we did not have to walk. I looked up at the stars and the moon, a quarter slice. I breathed a deep sigh; at least these did not change. Nor God, I thought, amazed and ashamed that I had not thought of Him at all these last days.

I prodded Almaz. She did not waken.

Gently I took her hands, folded them together, with my own covering them, and I said a prayer for us both.

Weizero hung on the edge of life for days and days. They put her into a tiny hut on a low bed of strings, with a hole cut out for her body wastes, and a pot below, which sometimes someone changed. They stuck a needle in her arm, and above it hung a sack with water in it, and she lay motionless, but at least breathing.

We received some grain and a bottle of oil. I also got a small portion of powdered milk for Almaz. The oil and grain were soon gone. I used the empty bottle to collect our water when the truck came. When the truck did not come we went to the river, nearly dry and fouled by people and beasts. There was no other source. The American kept digging for a well; no water came up, and the others shouted at him, angry.

Hagos stayed nearby, wanting to be with Almaz. He talked to us constantly, explaining. Once when no food had come for four days, Hagos came to me.

"Desta, if you have something to trade, I know a man who will get us food."

"What does he want?"

"Money. Or anything gold."

"Where does he get the food?"

Hagos shrugged. "From town. Maybe from a truck. The food comes from other countries, I think. They are supposed to give it to us free, but," he shrugged again, "people like to cheat us, making money."

I gave Hagos one of my bracelets. With it he brought

us grain to last for a week. I knew Hagos also took a share; it didn't matter. What did I need a bracelet for? Still, I vowed to keep the last bracelet if I possibly could. I would want something in Jerusalem that belonged to my mother.

During the day we sat with Weizero Channa, and in between we looked for people from our Simien mountains; we found none. Where were the other Jews? we wondered, then realized we could not find them. They, like us, would be terrified to let it be known they were Beta Yisrael. Here, too, the others would accuse us of *buda*, maybe even of bringing the famine. They would kill us for sure.

One day after we'd been there a week or so, Melake went into the line at dawn, hoping to be taken to work. "Whatever they give me to eat, Desta," he told me, "I will bring half of it back to share with you and Almaz and Weizero."

"Are you strong enough to work?"

"I must try. Hagos said sometimes there is no grain for weeks. Trucks get stuck in the dust. Sometimes the food is stolen."

"Be careful who you talk to," I said.

Melake lifted his head. "I say nothing. I only listen."

Just after dawn, the work trucks rumbled into camp, raising storms of dust and an outcry from men begging for work. Melake was with them. Soon afterward he found me. His face was bloodied. One eye was sealed shut.

"The same thing follows us here," he panted. "Falasha. *Buda.*"

I grasped his arm. "You told them you are a Jew?"

"No. I said nothing. They looked at me. Somehow they knew."

"How?"

He sighed, turning his head to hide the bruised eye. "How do they ever know? They just do. The others will not let me work."

So we sat with Weizero Channa, watching her, praying for her. Someone must have heard us, though we kept our voices low.

"Beta Yisrael?"

A man dressed in a ragged white robe approached the hut. He had a full head of curling gray hair and a short gray beard. He told us his name: Itzhik.

"You are Beta Yisrael, I can hear your prayers," he said. I shook my head.

"There are many of us," he said, "and afraid to be discovered. But still we keep our ways. We must keep our ways. The redemption is near!"

I gazed at him. How could he speak of redemption in a place like this? Ten thousand people waited here: Some called it the gates of hell. And this man could still look at us smiling, speaking of redemption.

He said, "You will come to us." He pointed. "On that side of the camp—and scattered in many places—are our *tukels*. We try to keep them clean. Come to us. Tonight is Shabbat."

At the word "Shabbat," my throat filled. I said nothing until he had left.

"If we go to them," I whispered to Melake, "we become targets for everyone in camp."

"If we don't go to them," said Melake, "we remain alone. Without Shabbat or anything holy, we would be like Hagos."

"Like Hagos?" I stared at Melake. Yes. The little boy was wild, a camp child, belonging to nobody, unable to feel the difference between sorrow and joy, death and life. He had, indeed, led us by the hand to watch an old woman dying; he had taken us to a hut that was set afire with corpses inside, and as we stood there, numb, watching the flames burst up, Hagos clapped his hands and screamed out with delight, "Ha ha! What a blaze!"

I told Melake, "You are right. We'll go."

That night we crept to the place Itzhik had showed us. Beneath a small tent made of people's ragged cloaks and *shammas*, prayers were spoken, and those who knew the words by heart chanted the proper refrains. One man had a Torah, tattered and crackling with age. He read from it by the dim, smoking light, "The children of Israel are commanded to keep the Sabbath. Do not forsake this holy day which I have given you out of love."

"We are strangers in a strange land," said the reader. "But there have been others like us before, and saved. In Egypt. In Babylon. Then our people survived. Even if a multitude died, a remnant remained, seed for a new beginning. We are still the same. We are His children, to serve Him and obey the commandments. So we keep the Sabbath here, as our people have kept it from generation to generation."

Other Sabbaths followed, five, six, or seven. I don't know for sure how many; in the camp I lost track of time. But gradually I learned what we were waiting for.

For months now, a large rescue operation had been going on. Jews were found in the camps and at night taken away in buses, finally to be flown to Israel.

171

"How does it happen?" we asked in amazement, for we had seen nothing.

"It is all done in secret, with bribes, plenty," other Jews told us. "Almost every night fifty or sixty people are taken away in buses, then to the big city. There, planes come to take them away to Israel."

"And all in secret? In silence?" We could not imagine it.

"It must be secret. Of course, some officials of the camp know about it, but they look the other way. They are paid plenty for their blindness."

Gradually we learned these things: The government of Sudan could not admit to helping Jews. Sudan, after all, was a friend of the other Arab nations, and there is fighting between Arabs and Jews always. Still there are good people everywhere, good Sudanese who were glad to see somebody get out to safety. And there were others who did it for the money only. Some of them, too, were Jews.

"Don't trust that list maker," said Yagi, one of the Jewish men in whose makeshift *tukel* we held prayers. He pointed to a man in a long brown tunic, walking with his hands in his pockets. "Some take money from us to get on the list, then do nothing. Or worse. They sell our names to our enemies."

"I have no money," I said.

"Some take other things besides money," Yagi said, frowning darkly.

"Who is it that comes?" I asked Yagi.

"Asa. A saint."

"From Israel?"

"He is an Israeli now. Before, he too was a refugee."

Each day more information came our way, more tension.

"Another group got out last night."

"Who? How did they know whom to trust?"

"A man came. With a bus. His name is Asa. He is a good man. He takes risks for us, plenty."

"How does he choose, this Asa?"

"We don't know for sure. There are several list makers. They have to be sure you are Beta Yisrael, because the others would also like to leave this hellhole, go to Israel, you see, be taken there as brethren, and nobody the wiser."

"Christians would go? Even Muslims?"

"Here they are starving, isn't it so? What future have they here? No country wants them. Poor, diseased, where can they go? No, we Jews are the lucky ones. We have a land, and a people who want us. So, make yourselves ready."

Itzhik found us one day by the water truck, waiting for our portion. I realized then that he was the list maker, the honest one. Nobody saw his lips move, covered as they were with his *shamma*.

He let go a single word. "Tonight."

14

WE HAD TO MAKE OURSELVES READY. HOW DOES ONE GET ready for the redemption? For the coming true of a promise that is over two thousand years old?

A sense of quiet wonder came over me; I felt a terrible nearness to God—terrible, I say, because I trembled with every breeze, with the look of every pair of eyes. I felt Him everywhere around me, seeing and knowing. Strange, they called it the gates of hell, and it was horrible, and yet on that day I felt God's presence here, and I thought, hell is not a place forgotten by God: it is a place forgotten by man.

Almaz and I went to the putrid river to wash ourselves. The water was warm and thick with sand and mud. We had nothing else. Almaz was all scabs and sores and her ribs standing out sharp, and she was always coughing, like me. Her blouse had ripped open from the wires. It hung over her in strips. I threw it away. I took the skirt I had given her, brought it up from her waist to her neck and tied it there, so that she wore only one piece, but still there was so little of her that it was enough.

174

"But where are we going?" Almaz asked. She held my arm while she wiped her face with the other hand. It had gotten so that she would hardly ever let go of me.

"To Jerusalem," I said.

She made a strange face. "You told me that before."

"At least we are leaving here," I said.

"Well, how do we know the next place won't be worse?"

"It can't be."

"How do we know that man will take us to Jerusalem?"

"We have to trust someone," I said.

"Can we bring Hagos with us?"

"No. And you must say nothing to Hagos about our leaving. You promised!"

"What will he do without me?"

"Hagos will find a new friend. So will you, Almaz."

"How do we get to Jerusalem?"

"Buses will come for us. I have told you, Almaz. Someone bought buses to take us out of here."

"Who would do such a thing for us?" she exclaimed. "And how do you know they will really save us? Suppose somebody sells us as slaves?"

"Almaz, where did you hear such things?"

"It has happened," said Almaz, her face solemn. "Hagos told me. He knows."

"I won't let anybody hurt you," I said, hugging her. "I promise."

With a few twigs and straw and part of a cardboard box, we had made a shelter of sorts, round, like a nest, and no roof. I had laid my *shamma* over the top of it, and Melake's too, and we laid Weizero down in this place. I wanted Hagos

175

to have this little nest after we'd gone; I was afraid to tell him.

From the medicine of the magic needle Weizero Channa had soon grown strong enough to leave the hut and the little water sack attached to her arm. Still, her mind wandered. She sat in our little nest, and she nodded to herself, telling her dreams. Mostly she slept, then awakened and called out, as she did on this last day, too.

"Dan!" she called, and when Melake came close she clasped his hand and stroked it.

"I am Melake," he said. "Melake."

"Good boy, Dan," she crooned. "Soon we will see Jerusalem with our own eyes, soon. You must tell the *kess*. You must tell the *kess*. . . ." Then her voice trailed off, and she slept.

"When the bus comes," Melake whispered to me, always fearful of being overheard, "we must be there. We must be in the front. Last time they took only one bus full, that was all."

"Why didn't they return for more?"

"I heard the bus broke on the way."

"What happened to the people?"

Melake looked down. "They were taken."

"Where?"

He shrugged.

I reached for the knotted cloth that I still kept inside my dress. I put the bracelet around my wrist. One must have something beautiful take to Jerusalem.

I said to Melake, "Listen, if anything happens, if the bus breaks down or we are caught or anything . . . we must try to stay together. We must say that Weizero Channa is our own grandmother. We must never let them take her from us."

"Of course, Desta. We four are family now, and we will take care of each other, always. I will never forget that you sold your jewels for our food." Melake gazed at me, his eyes so full of feeling and lips parted, that I had to look away for the thoughts that suddenly flooded over me.

Weizero, suddenly keen and sitting upright, called my name. "Desta! Dan!" she pointed. "My children," she said, bobbing her head up and down. "Dan, how lucky you are with this woman for your bride. She is like Yehudit, our ancient queen."

Weizero gestured with her hand, waving. "One thousand men Yehudit led into battle!" Weizero Channa shrilled. "They cursed her, the Amharas, for generations, but they did not dare to attack us again. Ah, she was a warrior, a leader. What a spirit she was! And Desta . . . my child, you have brought us to Jerusalem."

"Soon, Weizero," I murmured.

I glanced at Melake. We had talked and talked about old Weizero—had a *zar* entered her somewhere in the desert, making her mad? Would the madness leave her when finally we got to Israel?

Long before evening we went out to the edge of the camp by some bushes and brambles, sitting with a small dung fire, as if we were cooking there and looking innocent. Darkness fell. Still we waited. No noise of anything came to us, no truck.

Then came Itzhik. I don't know why he chose us, but

he did. "I want you to be on that bus," he said. "You must go now, over there, and as soon as you see the bus, stand forward. Take the girl in your arms. And the old one," he said, nodding to Melake. "Try to keep together. We have tried to organize it, to persuade the people that all will be rescued eventually. But they are frightened and sometimes they panic, and we have to beat them back. There might be confusion, but stay together. Stay together, children! And bless you."

Itzhik was right; soon there was great pushing and confusion. A small beam of light fell upon us. I nearly screamed, remembering that other light and Dan's capture. Someone pushed me from the side, another from behind; I held my place.

"This baby is dying! I must get on the bus."

"Please, please, we have been here already a year."

Voices became strained, rasping. "Traitors, you promise us redemption and deliver us into hell."

"Take me. Please. I have stood here three times before— I suffer too greatly. Look! I have but one arm."

Still I held my place.

"Beta Yisrael?"

I was trembling so badly I could not speak.

"Yes," said Melake. "Four of us. We are *zamed*. We are together."

"Where are you from?"

Someone new was asking questions, checking a list.

Melake gave the names of our villages.

"And the *kess* there? His name?"

"Kess Dawit. Kess Haim," we said, speaking the dear names with a sob catching there.

Then came Itzhik's voice in the darkness. "Yes, yes, take them. I have sent them. Hurry!"

A group was formed, silent, throbbing; a bus stood in the deep shadows, half-concealed by brush. A white man waited at the door, dressed in dark clothes. He placed his hands on people's shoulders, counting, and he murmured to us, "All's well. Hurry now. Please be silent. All's well. Don't be afraid."

Too soon the bus was full, then fuller, with every seat filled, and people on top of people, standing so close together that there was no space for even a fly. Those remaining pressed around the bus; it heaved.

The white man spoke. His tone was weary, and he pleaded. "Stand back, please. I'll return. I promise you. Please be patient a little longer. We will come for you, all of you."

From within the bus I could see the hands reaching out, straining.

"Next time. Tomorrow. Stand clear, please, and let us go. We must take the children and these old ones; they are very sick. Be patient. We won't forsake you. I swear it!"

The man motioned to Itzhik. "Now! You must come with us tonight. I have saved a special place for you, Itzhik. You served here long enough, and so faithfully."

"No, Asa. I can't leave."

"Itzhik! I see you grow weaker every time I come. Look, we can send another man to make the selection. Come now!"

"Asa, I am the only one who can speak to the officials in their tongue. How can I leave these people here, without language?"

"You cannot save the whole world, *shmagile*," cried Asa. "You have done enough. Get in now, be quick."

But I saw the man called Itzhik slip away into the shadows, and then Asa pressed his way into the bus, pulling the one armed man along, too.

Now we were tight in this bus, flesh pressed to flesh, and the heat had come in with us, strong.

The door swung itself closed. I knew a moment of sharp fear. Melake beside me murmured, "Desta. Desta."

The bus gave a great groan and a shudder and a strange stink. Then it moved.

Through the darkness we lurched; only blackness and the smells, too, filled us completely.

I thought of nothing. And everything. I thought of all the people, swarms of people, sitting there on the hot, bare sand, and I knew that they would never get out. They would die there. I thought of Hagos, waiting all his life for the water truck, for the bottle of oil, for someone to speak to him, for someone new to drag through, pointing at the sights. "There! Look. Look. These are the shaking ones. Malaria. See?"

Why are they here? I could never really understand it. Again and again I asked the question. Once I got an answer. "They are the people nobody wants."

I thought of the workers; we saw them around the camp, always sweating, always working. We used to call all white people foreigners. Now I had learned they were not all the same. There was Franz from Germany, Olga from Sweden, Shirley from England, Juana from Mexico, Douglas from America. My favorite was this yellow-haired man, Douglas. He smiled. Sometimes he called out, "Hi, kid!"

180

I learned the words, and I answered back, "Hi, kid!"

One day Douglas left and did not come back. I looked for him. Hagos said he had left the camp, tired and sick, going home.

As we sat in the bus I thought about him with his yellow hair, and I wondered what it was like in his home—did he have a *tukel* like ours? Or did he live in a square stone house with a canopy stretched out front, and even a well in the yard?

I slept. Almaz upon my lap weighed a feather. I dreamed she floated up, up to the top of the bus, laughing down at me. I dreamed of the thousands sitting, sitting, covered with flies and with heat, then Almaz again, laughing as she used to do, and Joas, standing tall with his military coat, and suddenly the coat was flung over my face so that I could not breathe. . . . and I awakened with the bus lurching to a stop.

"What? What?" A cry bordering on panic broke out.

"Don't be afraid," came Asa's voice. "All's well. It's only a checkpoint. Security. Be silent. Say nothing."

Sixty-five people in that bus with forty seats all kept silent. A baby whimpered. Instantly it was silenced, as the official came round to the driver's window, beamed in a light, then grunted out demands.

I heard the ringing of coins. Plenty.

Who pays? I wondered, holding my breath. And why? And who is this man, Asa, to come for us in the night?

Once again the bus moved through the blackness. Now I could feel that nobody slept; all sat with eyes wide open, bodies balanced, keeping the silence. For hours and hours we sat in the darkness with the lurching of the bus and the smells and the heat and the drumming of my own heart as I wondered whether this night would ever end. I thought of Joas, lying in his own darkness, and I felt a sob rising to my throat; with a swift prayer I shut it away again. There must be time, someday, to think of Joas. Of Dan. Of Aunt Kibret and Uncle Tekle, of Kess Haim, of all my people—but not now.

We stopped. Again someone came to the bus in a uniform with buttons glittering, and a cap. More words, gruff and short. Asa reached into a pack he wore on his back, said something, brought out many papers.

"Identity papers—yes, yes, students. They are all students."

I could make out some words; in the camp I learned a few in Arabic. Students? We?

Small green books were given to Asa.

"Travel permits," Melake whispered.

"Why can't people travel freely?" I whispered back.

Melake shrugged.

Weizero whispered under her breath, "Is this Jersalem?"

"Soon, Weizero," I soothed her. "Soon we'll really be there."

Again coins rang. I saw a wad of paper money being shoved swiftly into an open hand, then I heard a friendly slap on the side of the bus. "Very well. All clear. Get this bus off the road. Fast."

Of course, Aunt Kibret had been right. It would take money to buy our way out, for no matter what the law said or what a revolution stood for, there were always plenty of people willing to let you go; freedom has a price.

A strange thought came to me: How much does it cost for Almaz? What is the price for Weizero, Melake, and me? What are we worth? And who pays?

Asa went back to his seat. My eyes now were used to the darkness; I saw his shoulders stoop with fatigue. The one-armed man stood up, his one arm holding a strap. He swayed with the movements of the bus.

Nobody needed to tell us to be quiet. The silence was heavy in that bus, as everyone imagined things that might still happen to end this night ride in disaster. Maybe somebody in Sudan did not want Jews to leave; maybe they were afraid of offending the Ethiopian Dergue. Maybe the bribe money was not enough, or after being taken would be used as proof of our lawless flight. When things are done in the night and in secret, there is no way to be sure of anything.

Israelis wanted us to come to them. Well, the Israelis have enemies, plenty, Arabs all around who do not want them to take more people into their land to make more settlers, more soldiers, more lovers of Zion. Ah, the world is so large, I thought as we sped through the night. So large, and so many people in it, all wanting something. What is it they want? All I wanted was a bed to lie on, and for my stomach to cease its fiery cramps. And water. A sip of water, please. I held Almaz; I could feel her ribs. I could hear the rasping of her breath. I did not know what was wrong with her.

We traveled on, drove into a gate, down a long, dark, empty road. Almaz was asleep on my shoulder, her mouth open and teeth digging in. Suddenly Weizero was wide awake.

I saw her eyes gleaming, sharp; now she was in one of her keen times, noticing everything.

The bus stopped, something in it groaning loud. The door swung open with a hiss. Hands moved us out of the bus. Hurry. Hurry. My legs tingled and stung from sitting cramped so long.

We stood in darkness in a building all of metal, looking out to a vast field with tiny winking lights.

I felt someone touch my back. "Almost there," said a deep voice. Asa. I turned to look at him. He took Almaz from my arms, held her across his shoulder. "You must be tired," he murmured.

"Who are you?" I whispered.

"My name is Asa."

"But who sent you? Why do you come to help us?"

I saw his teeth, very white in a grin. "Why not?"

"Isn't it dangerous?"

"Living is dangerous." He gave a soft laugh.

People became restless. Some voices were raised. "What are we doing here? What's going on? I'm not staying in this place. Let me out!"

"Don't worry," came Asa's voice. "The plane is late."

Almaz awakened. "Plane?"

Asa set Almaz down. He had things to do.

"We're going on a plane to Israel," I whispered to Melake, needing to hear the words again.

Melake touched my hand.

Behind us the shed filled with more and more bodies, pressing close. More came and then more again, slipping in swiftly and silently, more and more, until the shed was full and some of us were pushed out the door into the cooler night to stand and watch the lights and the stars.

I whispered to Melake. "Who are all these people?"

"Jews," he whispered back. "Like us. Going to Israel in a plane."

People began to whisper now to each other, finding each other alike, Beta Yisrael, and starved for news. "Do you know Yosef from the village of T——? Do you know what has happened to the people of M—— lately? How are the crops over there? Did it rain yet?"

And stories were given now, swiftly and in bursts, like pellets falling out of a gun, telling things we did not want to hear, but needed to hear just the same. I wanted to cover Almaz's ears, but what would have been the use?

"In our camp," said one woman, "six hundred children died."

"All Jews?"

"Friend, a child is a child. Six hundred died in four weeks."

"We had not time to bury the dead in our camp," said a man. "We only heaped stones upon them. Couldn't say Kaddish, you know, because the others would come and kill us if they knew we were Jews."

"Well, we are the lucky ones, going to Israel in a plane."

"Who is doing this? Planes cost money—who gives money for the likes of us?"

"Someone—God has sent us deliverers in this time, in this time. Don't ask who—only praise Him!"

"Wait. We aren't there yet," said a woman, spitting into her palm for good luck.

I had seen a plane before, but high in the sky, like a bird. Very small. Now it came down upon us with a roar, loud and large enough to close up the sky, and I trembled so. But again we had to hurry. There was no time to be scared.

I know nothing about a plane, only that it roars, and it holds you back, hard against the seat, and then there is only blackness, and dim lights, and water comes in a little cup, water enough to quench the thirst that has lain in the throat so long.

Weizero Channa was sleeping, deep, in the seat beside Melake, and me beside him, then Almaz, we four together in a plane on the way to Israel.

First people were afraid to talk. Then food came. Rolls. Butter. Coffee. All of it was brought to us by women wearing soft clothes, so pretty. The plates were white and gleaming, and there were small papers to wipe the hands, and water, too. Plenty of water.

A voice came now from somewhere, loud and full. Asa. "My friends, now it can be told," he said, "and you will hear the full story in time. You are part of the greatest rescue operation ever made. We call it Operation Moses. For years people all over the world—Jews, Gentiles, Americans, Canadians, Europeans, Israelis—have been collecting money and planning how to get you out of Ethiopia. Of course, you yourselves had to make it happen. You had the courage to leave your homes, and the faith."

I glanced at Melake, thinking of Joas.

"All our work has been in secret," continued Asa. "This

plane was given in secret by a Belgian Jew. We have flown out in secret, with only a few officials knowing of this mission. Thousands of your people are already in Israel. Thousands more will be taken out of Sudan in the next few months, until all the Jews are out of Ethiopia and safe. The world does not know yet what is happening, but someday this story will be told. Now you know the truth. You were not forgotten."

Almaz looked ill; she held her stomach. Too much food, too fast.

The white woman motioned. Almaz would not go without me; I took her into a tiny room with many silver things in it, and a mirror. I did not know the girl who stood there. I touched my cheek. My hair. I never knew my face was that way. We looked and looked. Then we lifted up a lid and found a deep and shining silver bowl, but no place for Almaz's comfort.

"Can you wait, Almaz?" I coaxed.

"Yes. I can wait."

Something small and creamy white lay there.

"Look! It is soap."

We rubbed it on our hands, found water down in the deep silver bowl and dipped off the foam. Almaz laughed. I had not heard her laugh for a very long time. We did it again, again, until the soap was only a sliver and the silver bowl was full to the top with foam. A knock came at the door. We hurried out, back to the seats, our hands smelling sweet, back to the little water cups.

Everything can happen on a plane that happens anywhere else. On this plane a baby was born. We heard the mother wailing. We also heard the child. A cry of joy went up, and singing. On this plane, also, a woman died. We saw her carried out later, stiff, laid down in a box.

The plane came down somewhere. Asa said it was Belgium. He said we were not to worry; soon we would be on the way again, in another plane and flying to Israel. El Al. This plane had a name: El Al.

Flying to Israel. What magic exists in this world! I thought, next Aunt Kibret and Uncle Tekle will come through the night with Asa—yes, yes, it would happen. For the first time I felt a great joy and a certainty. For the first time I looked back down the time since we had started, and saw how far we had come.

I pressed my fingertips against the material of the seat. I looked up at the tiny winking lights in the wall. The woman in the pretty clothes covered Almaz with a blanket and gave me a smile.

I smiled back, then slept.

A roar. A bump. The plane was down. My head swam. Everything spun in circles.

Music came from somewhere, filling the plane. I will never forget that music. The notes were sweet. They flowed along the air and onto my skin, covering me, bringing shivers.

A voice came from somewhere, over the music.

"Welcome to Israel. Welcome, welcome to Eretz Yisrael."

We stood, moved out, I clinging to Almaz. Down those strange rails we went, and it was cold on our bare feet. People fell to their knees and kissed the ground, Melake among them.

Someone brought a chair with wheels for Weizero

Channa, and we hurried alongside. How did they know? Who arranged it?

Inside, lights shone like the middle of the day, while outside still the darkness held. There were faces, faces, more white faces that ever I have seen with so many smiles and hands waving, people crying and calling, as if they were our *zamed*, "Welcome! Welcome! Praise God, they are here."

15

WE WENT AGAIN IN A BUS, DAZED AND DROWSY, RUSHING through darkness, and the next thing I remember is opening my eyes in the morning in a small room, lying on something soft—a bed, with a mattress. Almaz slept beside me, tangled up in a blanket of dark material.

I got up to look for water. I went to the wall, touched it, and felt the hardness, remembering the mud wall of our *tukel*. This wall was white, shining, giving a brightness that made me blink again and again. I looked out the window, which also shone, but I saw no river or pond or water truck.

Other beds held other sleepers, eight of us, some girls and two mothers with small children. All were waking up now, blinking, coughing, confused.

"Desta, don't leave me! Where is Weizero? Where is Melake?" Almaz called. I went to her. Her face was very hot.

"I don't know. But hush, Almaz. We are in Israel!"

We opened the door and stepped outside, to see such

marvels. For too long we had looked upon desert sand. Now we saw green grass, trimmed and bounded with smooth walkways, flowering shrubs of bright red, yellow, and white. Everything gleamed so, even the walkways had tiny specks of silver embedded in them, and Almaz gasped, "Desta, the streets are jeweled!"

Almaz bent to touch the street with the palm of her hand; she laid her face against a bush with large, green leaves. Above, the sky was deep blue, and in the air we could catch breezes sweet with flowers I later learned were honeysuckle and orange blossoms.

A woman hurried toward us, arms outstretched, smiling, "*Shalom!*" she exclaimed. "*Shalom!*" It is the word for many greetings in this land—hello, good-bye, peace. Her lips were painted red, also her fingernails. From that moment all of us wished for such painting, too.

She pointed to her chest. "*Ani Ruth. Shalom.*"

We answered, "*Shalom, Ruth!*" laughing, happy to be speaking our first Hebrew word. We said it again, then to each other, "*Shalom! Shalom!*"

Ruth wanted to hear us say our names, and in turn we pointed to our own chests, and when it came to me and I called out, "*Ani* Desta." I am Desta. *Shalom.* Now that I thought of it, that first week in the camp in Sudan nobody knew our names, nobody asked.

Ruth motioned for us to follow her. Soon we were in a room with many shining bowls half-filled with water, each bowl in a little room with its own door.

Ruth pointed. She spoke.

We stared at her, wanting to please our new friend, not

191

knowing how. *"Shalom,"* we said, nodding and smiling. Yes, very nice. But where are the water jugs?

Ruth twisted her mouth, thinking. Then she stepped forward, and she took a little child from its mother, pulled off its bottoms, and sat it down over the bowl.

Well, there was a great smiling and clapping of hands, and laughter too, when the child did what it was there for.

So we learned.

Looking back, I wonder at the strangeness of those first days, and I will tell only a few things. The rest, the fullness of our new life here, that is another story.

Well, that first morning we saw water pouring out of the wall for our shower bath, and it was warm. Ruth gave us new soap, and special medicine for our hair, to let out the lice. The bathing in clean water brought such happiness to Almaz and me that we started to sing, but then Almaz went into coughing so hard that she could not stand.

Ruth gave us white towels to dry ourselves, and a bag for our clothes if they were too ragged. Most of us kept our *shammas*, just to have something from home; it is hard to give away everything on the first morning. We got new clothes—underwear, shirts, and a warm suit, blue jacket, and pants called a *training*. Each jacket had a thing we'd seen before. Almaz laughed and laughed, remembering, a "zipper."

On came the suits, until we all stood together, girls and women, laughing so to see each other beautiful with warm clothes, all alike. Shoes next, white and with bending bottoms and strings in them for tying. We all knew how to make knots from tying so much straw for our *tukels*, but Ruth was surprised and very happy to see it.

192

In our new clothes we went with Ruth to a large room, all gleaming with windows and bright tables. Melake was there! My heart leaped. I waved to him; he did not see me, for he was talking, talking with men. Israeli boys brought bread on large pans, and we ate. The bread was high and puffy, and no *wett* for it. We found pepper, shook it out upon the bread. Eggs came. We ate, looked for more pepper. The boys ran back through big silver doors and returned with more pepper, amazed to see how black we made our eggs. Nobody loves pepper as much as we do. Later at school, our counselors brought peppers, plenty, to our tables, and when we got money of our own to spend, the first thing we did at the market was to look for spices, hot and strong.

Every moment was already filled with learning. In Ethiopia men do not bring food, only women. Soon, even Melake would carry a tray and clean off tables, and I would be doing man's work, planting seeds and pulling weeds. From the first moment, the excitement was from this newness, needing to gather and taste everything that these white Jews were doing, for haven't we waited so long to become one with them? Later, there were sorrows and disappointments, too. Jerusalem is not heaven. But that is another story, and one thing I know: For me this is my home forever.

Now I looked around the room. How fine we were, dressed all alike. Not so much coughing anymore, either.

Some of the people did not speak. Perhaps they had forgotten how. Or, like Weizero Channa, a madness had come to them from the days in the desert and then the days in the camp. At least Almaz and I were only thin, and we had gotten used to the cramps.

Soon again we were moved, with many people to guide us, smiling and touching. Israelis, I thought, like to touch and to smile. I had not been smiling much; now I would learn it again.

A man, black like us, spoke to explain. We would all see doctors now, to get pills and perhaps even magic needles. Some very sick ones would go to a place for healing. Hospital. We were very afraid; I have heard of such healing places. In them, people die.

We went to the doctor together; Almaz clung to my arm. With the doctor was a red-haired woman wearing a bright yellow sweater. She spoke Amharic a little, sounding funny, but I could put the words together.

"How old is this small one?"

"Nine," I said. I know the years of Almaz, because they are the same as my mother's death.

She told the doctor. The two looked at each other, eyebrows up. The doctor plugged something into his ears, laid it to Almaz's chest. I thought it was a magic thing to pull out the cough that has lived inside Almaz for so very long.

The two spoke together swiftly. Then the woman said, again in the funny, flat Amharic, "This child is too thin. Much. She needs special food and care. Maybe we should take her to . . ."

"You cannot take her," I said, firm and fierce. "Never."

Almaz clung to me, began to scream. "No! No! No!"

The doctor put something onto a paper. He and the woman talked, talked, while still Almaz screamed and began to tremble and kick.

"Enough wailing!" the red-haired woman said, her voice

sharp. "You and your sister will be together. Always. You will go to school together, and also your *zamed*, the boy Melake. And the old one, the grandmother, will get special care. You can say good-bye to her before you leave, and you will see, she is being cared for, plenty. Don't be afraid. We will give Almaz the magic needle now, and medicine to take every day."

Almaz became quiet again, puffing and sniffing. The woman gave her paper, soft and white.

Almaz stared.

The woman pointed to her nose, took the paper again from Almaz, began to wipe.

Now this was something new, and we did it to Almaz again, then watched as the woman did it to herself, making a sound, and the doctor was smiling, shaking his head. So another thing we learned, about papers and noses.

The red-haired woman put two small boxes into my hand. "The pink pills are for Almaz," she said. "Three times every day. The white pills are for both of you. Eat one every morning. Do you understand? Will you do it?"

"Yes. Thank you, Weizero."

Almaz was happy to get the magic needle. Of course, we thought it would pull out her cough right away, and make her fatter, too. This did not happen. But after a few weeks in Israel I saw Almaz changing, getting well. The same with me. One day I woke up, and my body was light again, without the weight of pain. The cramps disappeared, the fever, too. Until then, I had not known we were so sick.

Well, I put the pills into the pocket of my new suit, and suddenly I felt too weak. My head went light, my body

195

hot, then cold, and my stomach sour, churning.

"Desta? Desta?" The red-haired woman came to me. I put my head against her, breathing deep, deep.

It was the strangeness hitting me, you see. Because everything here was too new—hard, thick walls, floors that snapped when you walked on them, everywhere the lights, lights striking the eyes and doors opening, all looking the same, but with different things behind them. How would I ever learn what lay behind those doors?

I had expected something else.

I found myself speaking in a choked tone. "I thought . . . in Jerusalem there would be prayers. And singing, plenty. When are the prayers? Where are the synagogues?"

The red-haired woman stroked my head, so tender. "It is all too much for you. Soon it will be clear. Don't try too hard; it is only your first morning. There is a synagogue at the school where you are going. Also prayers and songs, plenty. Ah, Desta, you will be happy there. You and Almaz and Melake. It is called *Gan Tikva*. Garden of Hope."

Still dazed, Melake, Almaz, and I sat in the car, speechless as the scene rolled out before us. We had said good-bye to Weizero Channa, who lay in a room with four other women, all being tended with food and medicine. Weizero kissed us and wept and said, "Don't forget me, Desta! Dan, you must come to me on Shabbat."

It was hard to leave her.

Someone sent a car for us, with words painted on the side. We sped along flashing roads, past farms and factories, with the sparkling sea now and then visible, and strange trees

196

with waving fronds, houses with red tile roofs, and everything so neat and clean. No wild animals grazed, no baboons, elephants, or wild cats, and no *tukels* or tents. Everything was trimmed and controlled. Even the distant hills seemed peaceful and quiet.

Our driver spoke no Amharic, but he did say *"Shalom,"* and pointed to things for us to notice. But it was all too much, and soon we fell asleep, still exhausted from our trip the day before.

Suddenly I realized the car had slowed, and we were on a long tree-lined road, with houses on either side, small and pretty, a dog or two playing in a yard, a child on a swinging seat. The driver leaned out the window. An old man came out and opened the gate. We drove through. Tires crackled on the road, and now I saw fields and trees, more and more roads leading to low cottages with red roofs, painted the colors of pale flowers.

"How beautiful!" Almaz gasped.

"Gan Tikva," said the driver, waving to the woman who hurried out to greet us. Dark-haired, smiling, and wearing a jeans skirt and a red sweater, she came with her arms extended and drew us to her as if we were *zamed*. This was Lisa Pardin, the wife of the rabbi who was director of Gan Tikva.

Well, what can I tell you about Lisa? She was a mother to us, bringing medicine for our cramps, salve for our scabs and sores, giving us milk and small biscuits in her study, then wiping our faces when we began to sweat again from the old fevers, and crooning to us in tones we understood, even though the words were different.

Lisa spoke not a word of Amharic, only Hebrew and

English. But her hands and her eyes and her smile were enough.

Lisa took us to the dining room, full of chairs and tables, and many windows, everything gleaming. There we met our new friends, Ethiopians, a boy called Josef, a little older then Melake, and two girls, wearing the school uniform, a jeans skirt and light blue blouse and a sweater. One girl was small, like Almaz, and her name was Sarah. The other was my age, Rachel.

As soon as they saw us both girls let out a cry of joy, as if we were family and they had waited for us.

Lisa spoke to the girls. Then she left us.

Someone had saved supper for us. Our new friends brought our meals on trays. "You will get used to it," they said, laughing when we made strange faces at the new vegetables and sauce, and wanted to eat only rice and bread. "Taste it," they begged, of the dark cake cut into small squares. "It is chocolate," they said.

We tasted, but could not eat this sweetness, so we gave it back to our friends, and they ate with pleasure, laughing and saying, "Remember when we first came? How we hated chocolate cake too?"

Josef had been here for six months, Rachel and Sarah for four months. My friend Rachel was a serious girl, and very pretty, with full curls all over her head, and a round, fine, strong face. I liked her at once. She told me she had two sisters, so she knew the feeling between Almaz and me. Rachel's sisters were not here with her; later I would learn her story.

She and Sarah explained their strange names. "We have chosen Israeli names. Most of the boys and girls do. You can if you wish—but you don't have to think about that yet."

Rachel took us to our sleeping place in one of the cottages. We four would be together, Almaz and Sarah, Rachel and I sleeping in four little beds in an alcove, and beyond these stood four little desks with chairs, then a washroom all our own, with a sink and toilet and shower, and plenty of soap.

"These desks are just for writing letters or reading," Rachel explained. "We study in the library every afternoon and evening. And we have free time from two to four."

"Free time?" asked Almaz. "What is that?"

"Time to play or rest," said Sarah. "Sometimes we have music. Or we lie on our beds here and tell stories."

Never had I seen a room like this. Never had I even dreamed it.

"Tomorrow you'll go to school," Rachel said. As I sat down on my bed I looked at everything, my head spinning. "You'll be in the first class, learning Hebrew, how to read and write and speak. As soon as you learn, you will go to another, higher class."

"You already speak beautiful Hebrew!" I exclaimed. "How have you learned it so fast?"

Rachel smiled. "You'll learn it too. Really, I am not so good. But I try."

Sarah opened a door in the wall, showing shelves. "A closet," she explained to Almaz, showing clothes neatly folded, shirts, dresses, sweaters, pants.

"We never had something like this," Almaz said.

"These shelves are for you," said Sarah gently. "You will get clothes, plenty, even dresses for Shabbat. You will get some tomorrow. And pretty shoes."

"I know it all seems strange now," said Rachel, "but

by next week you will know everything. Trust me. I felt like you do. Now, this is my home. In the morning we have prayers, girls apart from the boys. Then breakfast. We clean our rooms, put on our school skirts and blouses, and then the teachers teach us all day, Hebrew and things we must know, about cooking food and going to market, about taking a bus, about money and . . ." Rachel laughed. "That is enough for now, Desta. I see you are nearly asleep."

That night, although she had her own bed next to mine, Almaz crept in with me. Gradually she released my arm in the night. Then she moved into her own bed. Day by day during those first weeks I watched Almaz getting stronger, smiling more. When at last she left my side and went around the village with Sarah and other friends her age, I knew Almaz was really getting well.

How can I ever say enough about the wonders? To sit in a classroom and hold a pencil, to make marks on paper, to learn new words for familiar things, and new objects for old words—all this was a miracle. We had books and paper and time for music. And there was a shop for painting and other arts. My counselor, Rifka, gave me clay.

"Make whatever you like," she declared, smiling.

"At home I made water jugs," I told her, using the new words haltingly.

"Here you can make anything you want, Desta."

I broke off a small piece of clay and worked it soft. I rolled it round, round for the head, then another chunk for the body, and as I worked I lost my thoughts and my sense of time, all ideas of past or future. I molded arms and legs, then curls for hair. This was what I wanted to do, what I wanted to make—a mother holding a baby on her back, her eyes large and hair curly, her mouth open in a song. When it was time to close the shop and go to bed, Rifka came and looked at my small clay people. She laid her hand on my shoulder.

"You have great skill with the clay," she said, smiling.

I smiled, too. My heart was filled with pride.

"May I keep these here? To show the other children and all the teachers?"

I nodded. "Yes, yes. Oh, yes."

That first week Rachel and Sarah took Almaz and me to a special room with shelves and games and chairs. On a table stood a box, shining and pale.

As we stood there, several other girls came in, Rifka and Lisa, too, smiling as if they were waiting for excitement.

"What is it?" I asked Rachel, so proud to be speaking the Hebrew, *"Ma ze?"*

Rachel smiled. "Television."

I shrank back, doubtful, scared.

"It won't hurt you," Rachel said. "Watch."

Well, the next moment there came a picture, moving before our eyes, and words and songs and dancing! Moving! "Oh, God in heaven," I called out, looking from Rachel to the others, to the counselors and back to the box, the magic box so amazing that tears came to my eyes, and now I saw all the others, too, weeping with me and Almaz as we discovered this wonder.

The other wonderful thing was the telephone. We quickly learned how to put in our tokens and to call Weizero at her home, to hear her shouting, "Where are you? Are you here in Jerusalem? When are you coming to see me? When? When?"

Well two big things happened, both close together, that changed everything.

All of us had our worries, though we tried not to talk of them. Not a single child in the village of Gan Tikva had come with both parents. Most had lost somebody along the way. All had *zamed* and friends left back home, and for them we prayed morning and night. We consoled ourselves: Surely they would come to us soon. The planes were still flying, people were still sending money, men like Izhik and Asa would not stop until every last Jew was saved. Operation Moses was our hope.

One morning, just after breakfast, during the time for announcements, the terrible news was told. Our director, Rabbi Pardin stood before us, his hands clasped, his face strained and serious.

"This morning we have heard the sad news," he said, "that Operation Moses has stopped."

A single cry swept through the dining room.

He continued. "Word of the rescue leaked out. Newspapers all over the world printed the facts, that thousands of Ethiopian Jews have been smuggled into Israel. The government of Sudan has halted all emigration. The government of Ethiopia has done the same. Nobody can leave. Some who helped the Jews escape have been imprisoned. Or killed."

Not a word was spoken. We were stunned with grief. Closed? Ended? We were like people shipwrecked and floating in the ocean, waiting for help, cut off now, maybe forever.

Wordless and in accord we all left our breakfast there

on the plates, and we made our way to the synagogue building, where together we prayed. It was the wailing, weeping funeral prayer that our people have known since the beginning of our exile in Ethiopia. Lisa, the rabbi, and the counselors rushed in, terrified and upset. Still we wailed and wept and prayed. We did not stop, and we did not leave through lunchtime.

Rabbi Pardin came to us, very troubled. "Children! Oh, please, don't grieve so. What is it you do in your country when tragedy strikes?"

"We go to a high place," said one boy, the son of a *kess.* "There we fast and we pray."

"In Zion," said the rabbi, "the highest and the holiest place is the Western Wall of the old temple. Listen. I will take you there to pray. We will hire buses, and you shall pray for your *zamed,* and then you must break your fast, because you need your strength. How many of you would like to see the Western Wall?"

All hands went up. We could hardly control ourselves, even here in the synagogue.

"We will go to Jerusalem. Surely there your prayers will be heard, and we will have done all we can. In the meanwhile, you must eat your food. You go about your work and study your lessons. Agreed?"

We went in buses the next day, all the long way to Jerusalem, singing.

Rachel and Melake, Almaz and I had talked to Lisa. We wanted to see Weizero Channa, and to bring her with us to the Western Wall.

Lisa arranged it. We were taken specially to Weizero's

small apartment, where she lived with three other women, two white, one Ethiopian like her. She walked with a cane, wearing the new clothes, dark skirt and blouse and sweater, and even a shawl for her shoulders.

Oh, how we kissed, again and again, and she told the other women, "These are my *zamed,* my grandchildren. Aren't they beautiful? But you look wonderful!" she cried. "Happy and healthy, how beautiful you are!"

Melake and I looked at each other. It did not matter that Weizero Channa was a little unclear about how we were really related. After our travels together, who could be any closer than we?

"But I have a surprise for you," she said, and there was a gleaming in her eyes. "Dan is here."

Weizero Channa reached out her hands, and we thought that again the *zar* had puzzled her mind, so that she said *Dan* when she meant *Melake.* But in the next moment the door opened, and there he stood. Dan.

I screamed. I flew to him and kissed him again and again, held him close, held him far, kissing, kissing one cheek then the other, then stepping back to let Almaz get her kisses too, before Melake and Dan embraced like brothers.

My breath felt caught completely; I could not believe it. But there he stood, tall and gleaming so, wearing the same training we all had now, and a fine blue shirt, and on his head, a cap.

Well, there was time to talk at least a little, to hear the story. For four weeks they had kept Dan in prison in a small, stinking jail near the border. Every day they pulled him out. And they did things to him. I cannot tell you; my heart breaks.

They shouted that he must confess; he was a spy from Israel, they said, working to smuggle out Jews. After four weeks they gave up and took him in a truck half way up the mountains, saying, "Go home. If you try to escape again, we will kill you."

What to do? Which way to go?

"I thought I might go back home to find my father," Dan said, standing before us, hands outspread. He wore his old *shamma* on top of the new suit. "Then I thought, what if my father is not there? I am already halfway to the border. If I give up now, I might never get this far again. So," he shrugged, "I decided to go on. To Zion."

"But how did you get out of Sudan so quickly?" we cried. "We heard they have stopped the flights, and nobody can leave anymore."

"I was in God's hands," Dan said simply. He smiled. He was looking straight at me. "I was one of the lucky people, one of the last lucky ones to get out before the end. And here I am. Five days already, five days ago I became an Israeli."

I looked at Dan, saw the strength in him, saw also those marks of suffering that cannot really be described, but which the heart sees. Dan, I thought. My brother. And in many ways it was so; I had lost Joas, and now, here was Dan.

For those minutes I forgot my old fear. Suddenly it came back to me with a jolt. We had made an agreement. I was still his betrothed. I looked from Weizero Channa to Melake, then to Almaz. There was nobody here to speak for me, no father, uncle, or brother. Well then, I thought, taking a deep breath, I must speak for myself.

I raised my head and looked at Dan, fully. "Dan," I said, "we both remember what was spoken in Ethiopia. That we had planned a certain future. And promises were made."

"Yes," said Dan. He bent toward Weizero Channa, hoping she would speak for him, but we all knew Weizero no longer had her strength or her full reason. "We must talk about this, Desta," he said. "Maybe we should find a teacher or a rabbi or . . ."

"Maybe we can talk about it together now," I said, "with our *zamed* here to listen. I think," I said, and my heart was fluttering, though my voice was strong, "I think it is not right for us to marry. At least, not now. We are in a new land now, with new promises."

Dan started toward me, his eyes wide, and for a moment I thought he would answer in anger and shock, reminding me of my duty, of all he had suffered and sacrificed for me and for Almaz. Instead, he started to smile, then almost to laugh.

"Oh, Desta," he said, looking round to Melake, shaking his head. "I have been so troubled over this! I wanted to do my duty, and I felt that you . . . you expected and wanted . . . that is . . ."

"So it is settled," said Melake. "You can both study and put your minds on the future."

"Exactly," said Dan, beaming.

I pulled Almaz close to me, hugging her.

Weizero Channa raised herself up on her walking stick, and she called out shrilly, "Dan, Melake, Desta! I have not yet seen Jerusalem, and you stand here, talking, talking, like clucking old chickens. I have not so many years left that I can spend all my time with words about weddings and futures and such."

"You don't think it wrong of us, then, Weizero?" said Dan, bending to his grandmother, to give her a kiss.

"I think nothing," Weizero snapped, "except that you promised to take me to the Western Wall, to feel the heart of Zion."

"Let's go then," we all said, and we made a group together, Almaz, Melake, Weizero Channa, Dan, and I, with a taxi to take us to the old city.

Dan wanted to carry Weizero. She waved her cane. "I will walk to the Western Wall," she said firmly. "I will walk on my own two feet no matter how long it takes me to move up this hill."

So we walked, very slowly, up the long hill until we saw the Wall.

16

ALL MY LIFE, JUST AS I HAD HEARD ABOUT JERUSALEM, THE holy city, so had I heard about the wall, holiest place for a Jew in all the world. Still I was not prepared. How could anyone know the feelings that would gather here, at the wall?

Across a vast courtyard of stones worn smooth by millions of feet, we walked, Dan and Melake, Weizero Channa, Almaz, and I. Our footsteps were silent, as if held into the stones by some ancient longing of the earth itself. The stones had waited. The earth had waited. The time and the place had waited through all eternity for this moment. So it seemed.

There were other people, women and men, their numbers lost in the vastness of this place, and in its memories. Men went to one side, separated by a screen, women to the other. They moved slowly, as if returning into a long sleep and a dream from which they had been awakened against their will.

I moved with them, Almaz behind me, and somewhere beside us Weizero Channa, but I didn't know or need to know, for this is a moment when each Jew comes alone.

Slowly I approached the wall. High are the stones, and worn with time, the color of ochre, the color of dull clay with a hidden haze of gold. I leaned back my head to gaze at the top of the wall, to see the huge stones that were cut and carved and carried to this mount over two thousand years ago. Wars have raged here, but still the wall stands. It is the wall of our ancient temple, built by the captives who returned from Babylon to reclaim Jerusalem once again as their home. Only this one wall, the Western Wall, remains, for the temple was destroyed again by Roman armies. But this wall remains. And this wall I approached, my hands clasped, my eyes upon the stones.

I felt movement around me. Other people. I heard their breath, their weeping. I moved nearer to the wall, my eyes fixed upon the stones and their faint golden hue and the tufts of grass that grow between them, tiny weeds clinging there between the stones, the way a Jew clings to hope.

I thought of Joas, and I murmured a prayer. I thought of Aunt Kibret and Uncle Tekle, of Dan and all the others, and I prayed for each of them. Above, I saw the white birds flying about, dipping back to the wall, then out to the sky, fluttering back and forth, always returning.

I moved closer, closer, my eyes moist with a strange haze, and all feelings gathered here, until I could no longer see, but reached out with the palms of my hands, laid my hands flat against the wall, and then my whole body, my cheeks and legs and chest, and as I stood there embracing these stones, I trembled.

Like a leaf in the storm, I trembled, like a tree in thunder.

And while I clung there I felt a presence pouring through

me, and then a single thought came to me, "Here I am! Here I am!" for it is said that God calls every person to account, "Where are you?" In this moment I answered, "Here I am!"

I stood, trembling so—how long? How long?

I emerged at last, empty of tears, full of Someone who had enfolded me and answered, *"Desta, I see you."*

I had returned.

EPILOGUE

Operation Moses is a proud fact in the long history of the struggle for freedom. Between November 1984 and January 1985, some eight thousand refugees were saved in a secret airlift from Sudan to Israel. At this date some ten thousand black Jews are still locked away in remote mountain villages in Ethiopia, forbidden to join their relatives in Israel.

November 1986

SELECTED BIBLIOGRAPHY

Books
Doresse, Jean. *Ethiopia*. New York: G. P. Putnam's Sons, 1959.
Europa Publications. *Africa South of the Sahara* 1984–85. London, 1984.
Kessler, David. *The Falashas*. New York: Schocken Books, 1985.
Lord, Edith. *Queen of Sheba's Heirs*. New York: Acropolis, 1970.
Messing, Simon D. *The Story of the Falashas*. New York: Balshon Printing Co., 1982.
Parfitt, Tudor. *Operation Moses*. London: Weidenfeld and Nicolson, 1985.
Rapoport, Louis. *The Lost Jews*. New York: Stein and Day, 1980.
Rapoport, Louis. *Redemption Song*. New York: Harcourt Brace Jovanovich, 1986.
Schoenberger, Michele. *The Falashas of Ethiopia: An Ethnographic Study*. June 1975. (Doctoral dissertation for Cambridge University.)

Pamphlets, Magazines, Newspapers
Caputo, Robert. "Ethiopia—Revolution in the Ancient Empire." *National Geographic*, May 1983.
Caputo, Robert. "Sudan: Arab-African Giant." *National Geographic*, March 1982.
Jerusalem Post, International Edition. Numerous articles, 1985–86.
Jewish Agency Youth Aliyah. *Bulletin*. Edited by Dr. Nadine Caspi, June 1985.
Jewish Agency, Israel. *A New Mission for Youth Aliyah*, Youth Aliyah Pamphlet. Edited by Dr. Nadine Caspi, 1985.
Jewish Agency, Israel. *The Strength of True Partnership*, Immigration and Absorption Department Pamphlet. Edited by Ora Donino, 1985.
Lesau, Wolf. "The Black Jews of Ethiopia." *Commentary*, 1949, 216–24.
May, Clifford. "The Famine Workers." *New York Times Magazine*, 1 December 1985.
Powers, Charles. "Ethiopian Jews: Exodus of a Tribe." *Los Angeles Times*, 7–8 July 1985.
U.S. Government Printing Office. *Area Handbook for Ethiopia*, 1983.

Films
Anti-Defamation League of B'nai B'rith (producer). *Operation Moses*, 1985.
Eternal Light Program, National Broadcasting Company. *Falasha No More*, 1985.
Jacobovici, Simcha. *Falashas: Exile of the Black Jews*, 1982.
Levin, Meyer. *The Falashas*, 1973. Procured through Jewish Media Service, New York.

GLOSSARY

Beta Yisreal–House of Israel, tribal name of Ethiopian Jews
Buda–Evil Eye
Burr–Ethiopian coin
Debebkosh–Game of hide-and-seek
Dergue–"Committee," Marxist government of Ethiopia
Falasha–Stranger, a derogatory name for the Beta Yisrael
Ge'ez–Ancient Ethiopian language now used only in religious books
Injera–A round, flat bread
Kess–Priest
Margam Bet–House of Blood, or menstrual hut
Misvat–Special holiday bread made from wheat
Qat–An addictive drug in leaf form
Segid–A religious festival peculiar to Ethiopian Jews
Shamma–Shawl
Shifta–Bandits
Shmagile–Wise one
Shum–An official of the government
Sille–Hurrah!
Tedge–Local liquor made from fermented honey
Teff–Grain from which bread is made
Tella–Local beer
Tukel–Typical Ethiopian hut of twigs, mud and straw
Weizero–Lady, title of respect
Wett–Spiced stew
Zamed–Blood relatives
Zar–An evil spirit

N.B
Some Amharic words in The Return *have been Anglicized
for easier pronunciation.*